Dare to Love

by Laurie Ryan

www.laurieryanauthor.com

tions of this text, other than for review purposes, contact laurie@laurieryanauth or.com

QUALITY CONTROL: We strive to produce error-free books, but even with all the eyes that see the story during the production process, slips get by. So please, if you find a typo or any formatting issues, please let us know at laurie@laurieryana uthor.com so that we may correct it.

Thank you!

Acknowledgements

Publisher's Note

This is a steamy, emotionally charged contemporary romance featuring second chances, dangerous secrets, and a love worth risking everything for. With high-stakes suspense, forced proximity, and a fiercely earned happily-ever-after, this novel is perfect for readers who crave passion with bite.

Content Advisory:

This book contains explicit sexual content, strong language, violence, references to organized crime and maritime piracy, perilous situations, and emotionally intense themes including abandonment and betrayal.

From the author:

A NOTE FROM THE AUTHOR:

All good things must come to an end, right? Still, as I typed the final words on these pages, I found myself filled with melancholy. I got to know these characters so well and spent so much time in their heads that it's hard to let them go. They will always be with me, but now, it's time for new adventures. Stay tuned for more stories...

Laurie Ryan

DEDICATION

To all the writers out there who struggle to make this crazy business work.

Hang in there and keep typing those words!

PROLOGUE

"What do you say we blow this party, find some nice, quiet, uninhabited place, and get to know each other a whole lot better?"

Gail Grayson rolled her eyes, even as her ears tingled at the whispered words. That tingle wound its way past her brain as Aidan Walker settled an arm across the back of her chair.

She'd come to Mexico to help friends celebrate the renovation of a local village. Now, with the dedication behind them, the brightly painted gathering hall was overflowing with locals and visitors all bent on laughter and fun. Two hours ago, Gail had watched Aidan walk into the party like a predatory animal. He'd commandeered the seat next to her and hadn't left. Apparently, the man had trained his sights on her.

Don't think, her mind taunted in response to his question. *Just go. Be with him.*

It was hard to say no when she took time to appreciate the man whose hand traced the curves of her forearm. Brown hair, cut in a trendy, over-the-eye style, couldn't quite hide the

Irish in his green eyes. His lips quirked with mischief while he waited for her acceptance.

Gail's heart joined the chorus, its beat picking up with each slow, tortuous stroke of his hand along her arm.

She wanted to go with him. Lord, how she wanted to. Gail watched as his finger wound a lazy trail back and forth, and she almost gave in to the hunger that had her ready to explode.

Wide, muscled shoulders and a trim waist only added to the effect he had on her. Aidan Walker was hot. Not just hot, he was tossing flames that threatened to engulf her.

Gail resisted the urge to fan herself, but she made the fatal mistake of looking into his eyes. Little lines crinkled at the corners as he watched her, then he raised an eyebrow in challenge.

He knew how her mind was ogling him.

Damn it. This was not how things worked. She always had the upper hand when it came to flirting. Always. This seduction had gone on quite long enough and it was time to take back control.

Resting an elbow on the table, Gail cupped her chin and leaned closer to Aidan. She used her tongue to moisten lips she knew were colored the perfect shade of red and was satisfied to see his eyes dip to follow the movement.

"Isn't that what we're doing?" she asked.

"Huh?" A hint of confusion in his eyes was the only indication she got, but Gail knew she had re-taken the lead.

"I said,"—she paused, giving him time to focus— "isn't that what we're doing? Getting to *know* each other?" She used the hushed, sensual tone of her voice like a spell and Aidan's green eyes flared with a very gratifying desire as he responded.

"Not even close, darlin'."

Gail allowed her lips to curve into a lazy smile, even as her heart raced. "What would you call it then?"

Aidan's breath fluttered the short hair around her ear as he leaned in. "Foreplay." The word rolled off his tongue like melted chocolate. Deep, dark, and sinful.

Gail craved that bite of chocolate so badly she found it hard to breathe. Sitting back, she ran shaky fingers through her short hair and drew a slow breath.

Round one to you, Aidan Walker.

CHAPTER ONE

"Hello?"

Gail felt a gentle tap-tap on her head.

"Anybody in there?"

As her eyes re-focused, the skyline of San Diego coalesced into view. Damn. She'd been daydreaming again. Gail turned from the window to the woman beside her.

She'd been caught red-handed at it, too, if the smile on the woman's face was any indication. Luckily, her boss also held the distinction of being Gail's closest friend. Gail mumbled an apology and turned back to the conference table.

"Where were you?"

Green eyes flashed through her mind, gone as quickly as they came. "Just thinking."

Julia Thoralssen settled into a chair and patted Gail's arm. "'Fess up, my friend. Something's going on. You seem like you're in another world these days."

I am. A world filled with laughing Irish eyes and a smile meant only for her. Except that it was all in her mind.

A month ago, in Mexico for the re-dedication of a small coastal town that was near and dear to her boss's heart, she'd felt something click between herself and Aidan. Finally, she'd met someone who sparked a different kind of flame in her. They'd flirted outrageously and, well, some heavy petting had ensued before he took that phone call, chucked her on the chin and said he needed to leave. Gail sighed. She'd been certain he wanted a rematch. She'd given him her card, which had every scrap of contact information on it. Phone number, address, email, Facebook identity.

Everything.

"I'll call," he'd said.

Then, nothing.

Now, she ached with a regret that alternately added to her melancholy and pissed her off. She couldn't stop wondering what had gone wrong. Hell, she couldn't stop thinking about him, period.

She tugged on a spike of her short, dark hair while she tried to figure out what to say to Julia. Unable to come up with anything her friend might buy, Gail opted for a minimalistic version of the truth. "I'm fine. Just a little distracted."

"Honey, teenage girls staring at their latest heartthrob on the big screen are distracted. You are somewhere in space."

"I know. Sorry."

"Is it Aidan?"

Gail's head whipped up. "How the hell do you know about him?"

Julia threw her head back and laughed, sending strands of auburn hair flying. "It was kind of hard to miss. You two were rather, um, focused."

"It did seem like that." Gail looked out the window again. San Diego was worlds away from the small village of Tierra Bonita. Until a month ago, Gail had thought Julia nuts for setting up housekeeping there. Her husband's first wife had died in a mudslide and Julia and Hawk had spent a lot of time and effort rebuilding the village. That tall hunk of pirate she married was probably worth the exchange, but Julia was city born and bred. Until Gail had seen it for herself, she couldn't believe Julia would thrive in such a simplified lifestyle.

Tierra Bonita had convinced Gail, though. Julia was as happy working on a communal meal of local dishes as she was negotiating some high-powered contract in the boardroom. Where they lived didn't seem to matter to her friend as long as Hawk was by her side. And now they had a little one on the way.

Her friend had it all and Gail was ecstatic for her. At the same time, a small part of her wondered when it would be her turn. Instead of the forever thing, she was forever stuck in temporary trysts. The men in her life just didn't seem to want to stick around. Hell, maybe she wasn't meant to have the white picket fence.

Julia broke the silence. "He hasn't called?"

"Nope." Gail tossed her pen on the conference table. "No call, no email, not even a friend request on Facebook. I guess I made a real good impression, huh?"

"You always make a great impression."

"Yeah, that's why I'm still single, I'm sure."

"Don't do that to yourself. You have a lot to offer to some lucky guy. You just haven't met the right one, yet."

Gail's voice lowered to a whisper. "I kind of thought I had a shot at that with Aidan. It would be nice to find someone...to have something like you and Hawk have, you know?"

Julia's smile said it all as her hands settled on her growing belly. There was nothing better than being in love.

Would she ever know that with the same sureness as Julia? Gail was beginning to seriously doubt it.

"You know," Julia said. "You will find your man someday. I feel it like I feel this baby kicking. It's going to happen."

"Yes, but I wish I could find him before I'm old and gray and no longer interested in sex."

"You are aware that Aidan does a lot of undercover work, right? For the piracy division of the International Marine Bureau. Maybe he's in the middle of some covert thing?"

"He could've gotten word to me somehow. He would have if I'd been at all important to him." The whiny, nasal quality that settled in Gail's voice added to her irritation. She shook her head.

Julia's eyes mirrored the knowledge that she'd experienced Gail's frustration in her own life. Reading the understanding in her friend's gaze, Gail clamped down her frustration, unwilling to rain on Julia's happy ending.

She straightened and turned to the mass of papers spread out on the long table. "Well, enough feeling sorry for myself. It's time I got back to work."

As she left work that night, Gail decided she'd had enough of this pity party thing. How many nights had she spent sitting by the phone? How many times had she turned her blow dryer off because she thought she heard the phone ring? And how many nights had she slept with her cell clutched in her hand?

She was done with waiting around for Aidan Walker to call. So what if he didn't think she was worth a phone call. There were a lot more guys out there and one of them would turn out to be her Mr. Right. For now, though, she just wanted to hear pretty words, have someone pay her some attention, and ease the bruising her ego had taken.

She hadn't been out clubbing for weeks and suddenly missed it. Martinis and a little harmless flirting seemed just the thing to get her back on an even keel.

An hour later, Gail gave herself a final check in the mirror. Her short, almost black hair was in a state of artistic disarray. Her makeup looked flawless, if a little heavier than normal to hide the sleep loss. She'd chosen black capri pants with just a touch of flare at the bottom to showcase calves made even shapelier by the four-inch heels she added. The shimmery khaki-colored top left one shoulder free and accented her throat. The perfect chic casual outfit that said come-hither-but-I'm-not-trailer-trash.

Twirling, she grinned. Pappy, her gray Schnauzer, showed his agreement by bouncing against her leg. He jumped up on her black and silver satin comforter, bounded off to the other side and raced around the modern, stylistic furniture in her bedroom. He came to a stop in front of her, wagging his stub of a tail like a flag on steroids. Then he was off again on another circuit around the room. Gail laughed at his antics and, when he flipped over on his back, gave him a good tummy rub.

It seemed everyone was in a good mood tonight. Dressing up made everything better. A horn honked out front, signaling her taxi had arrived. Grabbing her form-fitting red leather jacket and matching clutch, Gail headed out for some well-earned fun.

Aidan Walker got off the elevator and the blast of noise infiltrated every pore of his body. Music spilled out of the doors in front of him, blaring some chart-topping song he fought to ignore.

What he couldn't ignore was the throng of people who blocked his entrance to the club. Altitudes was a twenty-second story open-air lounge in downtown San Diego that attracted players and seekers alike. Different colored light panels offset palm trees and the dark night sky. High tables and chairs mingled with couches and were filled with people networking and socializing.

He'd seen the likes before. Hell, he'd found company for the night in places like this too many times to count. He balled his hands into fists and reconnoitered the room. That idea was exactly what brought him to this place now. Gail was here.

Tired from an op he still needed to do a mountain of paperwork for, he'd found his thoughts too focused on Gail to concentrate. So he'd made the short hop to San Diego. Her apartment had been easy to find, but empty. Frustrated, he'd stopped by Hawk's place for a quick shower.

Getting information about Gail's whereabouts from Julia had been a problem. With a frown on her face, she'd vigorously protected her friend. Finally, after Aidan had explained he'd been whisked away on an emergency with no computer or phone or even privacy available, she'd grudgingly told him where Gail would be.

Out prowling at some damn club.

Obviously, their little flirtation hadn't meant much to her. At least, not like it had to him. Aidan frowned. He didn't care for the way he was drawn to this little pixie of a woman, but he sure as hell didn't seem to be able to stay away either.

His sharp eyes scanned the dimly lit bar as he maneuvered through the throng. He chuckled when he saw that the guys with girls all had beers in hand. And all the ladies sipped at a variety of colored martinis. Yep. He knew this scene well. Normally, he liked it, but not tonight. Tonight he was on a mission. He would find her, talk to her, then set her aside. That way, she'd be out of his mind for good and he could get on with his life.

He froze as his eyes settled on spiky hair that he would recognize anywhere. Hell, he didn't even *like* short hair on women. So why did his gut start churning as soon as he laid eyes on her?

Her back was to him, but her clothes hugged curves that had invaded his dreams. The woman had an ass meant for...

Aidan was hard just thinking about it.

Then he saw the shadow at the end of her table. Some yahoo leaned over and whispered in her ear. Blood began to pound in his head as he heard her lilting laugh answer whatever the man had said.

Calling upon years of undercover work, Aidan tamped down his annoyance and sauntered over to the table to place a proprietary arm across Gail's shoulder. At the same time, he nudged the guy back across the table.

"This one's taken, so why don't you go belly up to the bar, man."

He felt Gail stiffen beside him, but ignored her to deal with the jerk who mistakenly thought she would be easy prey. The man looked as though he would argue, so Aidan leaned toward him, placed his free arm on the table and took a few moments to flex muscles honed to a strength he knew this guy couldn't match.

The man got the message. He gulped some air, then turned and left without another word.

Which left Aidan alone with Gail at the table. He closed his eyes for a moment, taking in the spicy scent of her he'd missed. Which was why he didn't see the hand that caught him square across the cheek until it was too late.

"How dare you."

She pulled back to slap him again, but he caught her arm and pinned it to her side, pulling her against him. Leaning in closer, he got distracted by a whiff of her perfume.

Gail struggled to get free, but he held on tight. "Promise not to do that again and I'll let you go." His tone was low, but not low enough apparently. A glance across the room showed one of the bouncers he'd seen at the door walking intently toward them.

Aidan released Gail as Muscles reached them.

"You okay, Gail?"

She glared at Aidan, then spoke to the man. "Yes. Thanks, Jim. I can handle this guy."

She was on a first-name basis with the bouncer? Aidan looked the guy over. He was taller than Aidan and just as muscled. He showed it off with a tight T-shirt that sported some body-building logo on it. No way would Gail go for a guy like that.

"It looked like he was man-handling you," Muscles said. "You want me to boot his ass?"

Aidan's eyes narrowed as Gail took too much time to consider the request before finally answering. "No. It's okay. He's the friend of a friend."

"Well, okay. You just give me a nod if you want him outta here and I'm all over him." He glared at Aidan. "I'll be right over there by the door."

After muscle-man left, Aidan was able to concentrate on Gail. Before he could get a word out, she beat him to it.

"What the hell are you doing, marching in here and bullying my friends?" Her tone was sharp and the heightened color in her face lent credence to the fact that she was pissed. *Very* pissed, as a matter of fact. Aidan rubbed his cheek.

"I'm sorry," he said, trying to soothe her. "But you don't need some smooth-talker like that trying to score a night with you. And that's all it would be, you know. I've seen his type before."

Gail gave a single hooting laugh. "Yes. So have I."

Aidan combed hair off his face with his hand, settled on the tall bar-chair next to her and watched her stir her drink like it was some vile medicine. He braced a hand on the back of her chair to talk to her, but peripheral vision showed Muscles taking a step in their direction and glaring at him. Aidan pulled his arm back. Not that he couldn't take the man. He simply didn't want to make a scene here in the bar.

"Let's get out of here and go somewhere we can talk."

"No."

She wouldn't even look at him. What the hell was going on? Could she be that pissed just because he'd bounced some gigolo?

"Look at me," he said.

"No." Stubbornness was rooted in her voice.

With a glance to Muscles who was momentarily distracted, Aidan reached over and nudged Gail's chin up.

She was swelled up like a puffer fish. Only this wasn't fear. Her creamy skin was showing signs of blotchiness.

Oh, yeah, she was pissed.

Still, the hint of shimmer in her eyes said there was much more than anger going on here. What the hell had her so riled up?

"What are you doing here, Aidan?" Resignation overlaid the anger in her tone like the bass tones of whatever song the DJ was currently fading out.

Deciding it was time for a lighter vein, he pulled out his best Irish brogue. "Why, daerlin'. I've come to see yer bonny face."

It was a long moment before she reacted, then her face settled back to its normal loveliness as the anger melted away. Gail shook her head and chuckled. "That's the worst Irish accent I've ever heard. In fact, I think you've managed to mix Ireland and Scotland together."

"It's not one of my best attributes." He leaned in and winked. "I have others."

He stood up. "C'mon. Let's blow this place and go someplace where we can really talk."

Another hesitation, one that tipped his heart like the edge of a knife, was followed by a small nod. "Sure." Gail grabbed her leather jacket and purse and headed for the door.

Aidan paused as he watched her exit. He couldn't remember when he'd seen a backside that perfect. He was getting an erection just watching her sashay.

Damn, but he loved stilettos.

As she disappeared out the door, he hurried to catch up to her, tossing an I-win grin at Muscles as he flew through the door.

Outside, Gail used her cell phone to call a cab and tried to figure out why she was giving this guy any chance at all. He hadn't called her in an entire month! She should slam the cab door shut with him on the outside and never give him another thought.

She took a sidelong glance at Aidan while he scanned the street. He side-stepped a bench without looking at it, as if he were instinctually aware of everything around him. Gail knew he did undercover work and wondered if *alert* was his usual mode because of it.

His hair moved in the breeze and the longing to run her fingers through the strands welled up until she had to gulp to resist the urge.

She balled her hands into fists and warned herself yet again about being attracted to this man.

An elderly couple walked by, and Aidan's eyes crinkled as he smiled and greeted them. Gail wanted to touch those lips. Lips she'd only gotten a fleeting taste of in Mexico. Okay, so maybe she wanted to do more than just touch them.

No. She shook her head. He was the love-'em-and-leave-'em kind. She didn't need another one of those in her life. Better to get away now. To end this before it went further than her heart could handle.

She pursed her lips and prepared to explain her intention to get in the cab alone and go home.

Instead, she froze. He had turned her way and was staring at her with such raw need that it stole her breath.

Aidan moved closer and reached up to caress her cheek with the back of his hand. "I've missed you," he said.

Her tongue wouldn't form words. "I...I..."

One slight touch and her body and heart overrode her brain. She reached for his hand and held it against her cheek, leaning into it.

Aidan bent down.

Her lips parted.

He paused just before kissing her, staring in her eyes, showing her his need.

Then his lips touched hers, igniting a fire deep within that only one thing would quench. She snaked her arms around his neck and nestled into his body.

Aidan deepened the kiss and she parted her lips to let him in, relishing that first renewed taste of him.

Aidan groaned. His hands moved to her hips as he pulled her against his erection.

Someone coughed and he tore himself away and spun around. Gail could see the club's doorman watching them with keen interest.

Thankfully, their cab arrived at that moment and Aidan helped her inside. Joining her, he said "Where to?"

She stared at him for a long moment before deciding.

"My place."

CHAPTER TWO

Gail watched as Aidan's finger traced a tantalizing path between her breasts, winding leisurely along her stomach, then back up until his hand cupped her.

She wound both hands through her hair, arching her back in pleasure. Fresh from a love-making session that had rattled her world, the man seemed ready for another go round. She nudged her leg closer to him. Well, almost.

They both stilled as the *scratch, scratch* came again at her bedroom door.

"That damn dog of yours doesn't like me."

Gail laughed. "Sure he does. Or, at least, he will once he gets to know you. Pappy's a darling."

"Yeah, sure. That's why he bit my leg when we got here."

"It was a love bite. Really. He never broke the skin."

The noise beyond her door went silent and Aidan went back to working his way around her breast.

Gail sighed. She could drink this heady elixir again quite easily. The singles scene had been her playing field for quite a while now, yet Aidan Walker excited her in ways no one else came close to matching. With the body of someone who regularly worked out and no sign of any beer gut, she could get hot and bothered just looking at him. Flashing to the scene outside the club late last night, she remembered how accurate that thought was.

She brushed brownish-red hair off his face, a bit intimidated by the powerful desire she saw in his eyes. Yet she was also drawn to his hands which, at the moment, captured her complete attention. Quite certain he could have pummeled Jim, the club bouncer, with ease, those long sculpted fingers were now tender and gentle. This man rocked her in a way that, once she took time to think about it, would more than likely scare the pants off her. *Oh, wait a minute.* Gail smiled. *He's already managed that.*

"You're even more beautiful than I remembered," he said.

"Then...why didn't you call me?"

He stopped and propped himself up on an elbow to look at her. "Is that what all that attitude was about last night? Because I didn't call you?"

Gail's eyes narrowed and she started to move away from him, but he held her in place. She lay back on the pillow with a shrug of her shoulders. Between his ability to turn her on like flipping a light switch, and her lingering anger over the weeks of silence, relaxation was out of the question. "Not calling for a month doesn't exactly indicate an interest on your part."

He returned to doodling over, under and around her breast. "I got called away and didn't have a chance to contact you beforehand. Some of these...jobs...mean having no contact with anyone I know until it's over. I should have done something, though. Found some way. I can see that now. I'm...not used to thinking beyond myself and it was stupid. But trust me," he said as his hand teased its way to her other breast, "me being interested in you is a no-brainer and the least of your worries."

She gasped as he rolled a tip between his thumb and forefinger. "And what is it that I'm supposed to worry about, then?"

"If I were you, I'd worry about keeping up with me." He raised his eyebrows in challenge, then his mouth joined his hand, kissing trails around her nipple before he pulled it in deeper. He used his tongue like a master, swirling the tip, then sucking. Shards of desire ran straight to the vee between her legs, making thought incoherent.

"Mmmm," she purred. "That's nice."

He raised his head. "Only nice?"

"Well," she said, nudging him with her leg, "I wouldn't want it to go to your head."

"Ah," he said, the twinkle in his eyes giving notice. "I sense a challenge."

His hand replaced his mouth and Gail found concentration difficult. Her back rose to meet his hand with a will all its own.

"Beware, woman. I take dares *very* seriously."

Gail gasped. "You can take them as seriously as you want, as long as you keep doing what you're doing. Oh!" Words fled in the wake of the sensations that engulfed her.

She gripped his hair and pulled him in tighter as he put his mouth back to work, making good his threat to rise from nice to not-so-nice.

His hand moved across her stomach and lower, pressing her legs open. He stroked her, barely touching, with unhurried movements as his lips continued to tease her breast.

Ecstasy. Gail tried to reach for him, to reciprocate, but he stalled her by shifting so he could lean over her. He nipped at her other breast with his teeth.

At the same time, his hand tightened on her groin, one finger leaving a trail of fire.

He raised his head. "How am I doing so far?"

"Aidan!" she cried as he dove deep with his finger.

He pulled back then and she moaned with regret. It was momentary, though, as his mouth once again replaced his hand. He could use his tongue like an artist used a paintbrush. Delicate strokes here, hard and pounding there. It took only moments for her to climax in long, lingering waves of pleasure.

Afterward, he moved beside her, cocooning her in his arms.

Gail lay still for several long moments, waiting for her wits to catch up with the sated feel of her body.

"So?"

"Mmmm?"

"So, did I rock your world?"

The dare. He was talking about the dare. Gail chuckled as she looked at him. Her smile faltered when the laugh lines around his green eyes disappeared, edged out by the flare of desire. And something else. Something she couldn't quite figure out.

"Did you rock my world?" she repeated. "I'd say that's a distinct possibility." She propped her head on her hand and made sure he was looking at her as she spoke. "Now it's my turn."

He winked. "You're welcome to try, but I'm a hard act to follow."

"We'll see about that." She started with his face, tracing already familiar contours with her hand. Her lips joined in the fun, peppering his neck with light brushes of her mouth. As she kissed her way along his throat, her hand wandered down his body and took hold of him. There was no longer any question he was ready. Her hand moved again, circling his chest as she let the course hair glide through her fingers.

Then she gave his nipples the same attention he had given hers. Slow, slower, and slower still. Until he reached out and pulled her lips to his.

Gail allowed him to think he was in control for the moment, letting the kiss deepen and, in fact, almost giving herself up to the waves of sensuality his kisses elicited.

But it was her turn now. Breaking the kiss, she straddled him and he gasped as they connected.

Body to body. He nudged her with his hips, wanting inside. She made him wait and pushed hands away that reached to distract her.

"My turn, handsome," she said.

With a wide grin on his face, he acquiesced, twining his hands behind his head. "Do your dirtiest, ma'am." The fire in his eyes belied his relaxed air.

She squirmed, just enough to let him know the gauntlet had been thrown and accepted. Pleased to feel his body pulse beneath her, she renewed her interest in his chest, taking a nipple in as he'd done to her.

Aidan sucked in a deep breath.

In no hurry, she devoted time to both nipples, her own tight points aching from the movement across his body.

She wriggled again and this time his hands were on her hips before she could stop him.

He lifted her aside long enough to sheath himself with a condom. Then he plunged inside.

And howled his elation.

She moved slowly, savoring the feel of him. He cupped her breasts, stroking his thumbs over aching nipples. She felt the wave growing again and met each quickening thrust with her own need.

She'd lost control and didn't care a bit.

They crested together, falling into the chasm of satisfied fulfillment.

Wrapped securely in his arms, she slid into a drowsy prelude to sleep. As she fell deeper into the abyss, she heard his voice, low and filled with satisfaction.

"I win."

"Wake up, sleepyhead."

Gail stretched on her gray satin sheets like an uninhibited kitten, not quite ready to give up her warm, comfortable solitude, until a growl interrupted her reverie. She opened one eye, pushed her hair off her forehead, and stared at the man behind the rumble. "Was that the dog or your stomach?"

"My stomach." Aidan plopped down on the bed beside her. "Although your dog has done nothing but growl at me since I got up. I shut him in the guest room."

She could hear Pappy's whines now. High and pleading. She should let him out, but chose to stretch again. Maybe in a few minutes.

"I looked in your fridge. It's empty!"

Awake now, Gail protested. "It is *not* empty."

"A few condiments, leftover Chinese from some forgotten realm, and half a bottle of Chardonnay are not what I would call sustenance. It's mid-afternoon. I need food, woman." He pounded his chest with his free hand. "Feed me."

His attempt at severity was canceled out by the gleam in his eyes. Gail reached up and moved a lock of reddish-brown hair off his face. Lightened by striations infused by the sun, it was mostly straight and borderline fine. The trendy style suited him. It also said he was a player.

She frowned, recognizing how much she already wanted that not to be true.

"What?" he asked.

"Nothing," she said, pushing herself up.

Aidan settled his hand around her bare breast and leaned over to kiss her. He took his time, showing just how much he enjoyed her lips.

His thumb passed over her nipple and she shivered with anticipation and need. Steeling herself, she shoved him away.

"That's not going to get you fed, mister."

He jumped off the bed. "You're right." He turned to her, rubbing his hands together. "Want to shower together? You know. To conserve water?"

She laughed as she let the black and silver comforter fly, making a run for the bathroom while stepping over their discarded clothes and around a settee covered in ivory-colored leather that was her absolute favorite piece of furniture. "No. And just for your impertinence, I get first shower."

He managed a pretty damn good impression of a sad Pappy as she flew past. "Can I at least wash your, er, back?"

"Absolutely not! And let Pappy out." With a giggle, she closed the door behind her and leaned against it. It had been less than twenty-four hours since Aidan had shown up at the lounge. Now, he was seeing her at her worst, with no makeup and her hair going every which way. And she didn't even care.

What was wrong with her? She stared at herself in the mirror. Her hair was chaotic at best, nowhere near her usual artsy disarray. Her dark eyes still looked sleep-deprived. And her lips! She ran a hand across them. Puffy and well-loved. That was the only way to describe them. Even her breasts sported a slight rash from his day's growth of whiskers.

She looked like she had been making love for the past several hours. Something that, even though she hit the bar scene regularly, was a very infrequent happening for her. She sighed as she turned on the shower.

Gail knew she could get used to this.

Later, refreshed from their showers, she and Aidan wandered along the Embarcadero. She was used to San Diego's waterfront walkway, but knew it was hard to make sense of the diverse views. One side was all bay and boats, and the other direction, in stark contrast, flaunted the skyscrapers of a bustling downtown.

The afternoon crowd was thin for a Saturday and she was grateful. The Embarcadero, with all its shops, restaurants, and views of the bay, was one of the bigger draws for San Diego. Tourists visited by the busload.

Gail tried to pull Aidan into D.W.'s Pub for a veggie wrap, but he pounded his chest for the second time that day. "Me need meat, woman."

They ended up at the upscale-casual Edgewater Grill. Gail nibbled at her salad and watched Aidan treat his steak like a dear friend. He didn't so much devour his meat as relish every single bite as if it were the last steak he would ever eat. In fact, that seemed to be his motto. The man did everything with gusto, be it eating or making love. She thought back to the past several hours and decided that gusto was a very nice trait to have.

"You know," she said, "if anyone could turn me into a meat-eater, it would be you."

The twinkle in his eyes flashed brightly. "I will make it my life's goal to convert you, then."

Gail's heart raced at the possibilities.

Aidan signaled the waiter over and ordered the double chocolate fudge cake. He turned to Gail. "Would you like a piece? My treat."

"Oh, no. If I ate that, I would blow up like a blimp."

He dove into the dessert when it arrived and Gail watched him with jealous awe. "How come you're not the size of a blimp?"

"I don't really know, to be honest. Chalk it up to a good metabolism."

"A *really* good one, if tonight's any indication."

He took another bite and a cat-lapping-the-cream smile spread across his face. "You need to try this," Aidan said, holding out a taste.

Ready to protest, she found the cake-laden fork dangled in front of her too much to resist. While he held the fork, she closed her mouth around the chocolate with pleasure-filled slowness. Eyes closed, she took a long moment to savor the taste, licking her lips to capture any lingering morsel.

When she opened her eyes, it was to Aidan's stare. His mouth was open and he still held the fork in mid-air.

Gail arched her eyebrows. "Care to try that dare again, mister?"

The spell broken, Aidan laughed long and hard, which evolved into a coughing fit that took a full minute or more to control. "I think," he managed to squeak out, "that I may have met my match."

Gail patted him on the hand. "I'm pretty certain you have."

The check came and Aidan treated it like a natural occurrence as he paid for their meal.

In this day and age of speed dating, Dutch seemed the preferred method of payment by most men. Gail could not remember the last time a man bought her dinner.

Aidan Walker had blown right past "cool" on the possibility meter and was fast approaching "totally awesome." As she watched him tuck his wallet back into his khaki shorts, Gail wondered if this was some ruse or the real deal. She realized her hands were shaking. Tendrils of doubt worked their way into her heart as she wondered how much she could count on him being part of her future.

Aidan reached for her hand as they left the restaurant and walked the concrete walkway along the water. Gail saw him glance down at their intertwined fingers. It was almost as if he was surprised to find her hand in his.

He stared at their hands. Aidan Walker never held a woman's hand. Ever. What sort of spell had Gail cast on him?

The woman was a pixie. She didn't quite make it past the shoulder of his six-foot-two frame. He'd never liked short hair before, but her sassy, spiky cut worked. Really well. She must dye it to get that almost black color. Add in those brown bedroom eyes and a figure that he couldn't stop staring at, and he was a goner. He flashed to her sitting astride him, naked, with breasts that molded perfectly to his hands and a look of ecstasy on her face in response to having him inside her.

Damn. He was hard again just thinking about it.

It was even worse when she smiled, like right now. Shit, but she was the cutest damn witch he'd ever met.

A skateboarder behind them hooted his presence and Aidan pulled Gail against his chest as he evaded the kid. His eyes bore laser-like holes in the retreating kid's back. "Punk," he said under his breath.

"It's just a skateboarder, Aidan."

Shit. Now he was going overboard with the protection stuff. What the hell was happening to him? "Yeah. I know." Still firing glare-balls at the offending skater, Aidan didn't, at first, hear Gail ask him a question.

"Huh?" he said.

Gail repeated her question as they started walking again. "I understand you live in England?"

"Yes. That's where the IMB headquarters is."

"The piracy unit you work for?"

"The International Marine Bureau does a lot more than just deal with piracy. They handle regulatory issues and disputes, among other things. But my unit deals specifically with crimes that take place at sea, yes."

She frowned. "And that means you are, like, an operative or something? You go undercover, become these seedy character types so you can catch the bad guys?"

He chuckled and pulled her closer as they walked, wrapping an arm around her shoulder. "You don't have to make it sound so glamorous."

"It doesn't seem that way to me. It sounds dangerous."

"Listen, darlin'," Aidan said in his deliberately bad rendition of an Irish accent, "you're not to worry. I'll be takin' real good care of meself." He let her go and danced a little backward jig in front of her. "After all, I've go' the little folk on me side."

The smile returned to Gail's face. "Yes, with the red high-lights in that hair and those green eyes of yours, I'm guessing you are blessed by the little people. Still, the way you murder the Irish accent, they may just toss you out on your own, um, luck."

"It's the time in England, m' dear. It's corrupted me."

"You don't have a British accent, either."

They stopped to watch a sailboat coming into the marina as the sun set. Idyllic moments like this were what kept the tough memories relegated to the corners of his mind. And that was just fine with him. Aidan dropped the brogue. "Nope. Haven't been in England long enough. Hailing from good old California, there aren't any Brits rattling from the family tree."

Now why the hell had he said that? He never spoke about his past. It was his one rule. He'd have to be careful with this woman. It appeared she had the ability to charm snakes out of their venom.

"Where in California?"

"Oh, here, there, lots of places." He watched the horizon with a look he hoped belied any concentration on the conversation at hand. He'd bet a night in bed with her that Gail wasn't fooled. She knew he was dodging the question.

Thankfully, she let him off the hook, at least for the moment. "So, is that how you know Julia and Hawk?"

He laughed. "Actually, I met your boss for the first time the weekend I met you. I know her husband, Hawk, because I helped to arrest him for stealing several yachts."

"That's right. You know, that whole situation turned out great, with Hawk coming into all that money and being able to settle all his debts."

"And fund the village renovation," Aidan added.

"So, you worked with, um, Dion, right?"

"Yep. We worked a few undercover ops together." Aidan frowned as the flashes of memory peeked out from the far corners of his mind. They were so quick he barely had time to recognize them. First, Dion, shot in the back and knee. Then Claire, who took a bullet in the shoulder. He shook his head. It was always the bad stuff he remembered. So far, he'd dodged those bullets.

"The op we nailed Hawk on will probably always be one of my favorites. Because of that op, and meeting Claire, Dion retired from the division and took up philanthropy. So now I get to officially acknowledge him as a good friend."

"He and his wife seem nice."

Aidan's smile held the knowledge of a friendship bonded by time and circumstance. "They are both stand-up people."

Any more questions were forestalled when Aidan's cell rang. Gail's frustration morphed into apprehension as he wandered away from her to take the call. Was it the job?

She couldn't quite wrap her head around the fact that she was falling for a guy in this dangerous line of work. She didn't want to be the one waiting at home for a phone call or knock at the door, and had avoided dating cops and firemen for just this reason. Until Aidan.

His hello seemed neutral, neither business-like nor friendly. Still, the old fear filled her veins with ice. Could it be another woman on the phone? After all, she didn't know him *that* well. And he traveled a lot. He could have a woman in every port, for all she knew. Was she San Diego? And would he be like every other guy in her life and leave?

She watched his face transform from happy-go-lucky to all-hell-is-breaking-loose business. This didn't look like a conversation with another woman. It didn't look good, either. Gail sat down on a bench as the food she'd just eaten began to sour in her stomach.

He was going to leave.

Aidan flipped the phone closed and stood watching her for a long moment before joining her on the bench.

"I have to go," he said without preamble.

Gail nodded her head. "I figured."

They turned and walked in silence back to her apartment. Unsure how to tell him what this time had meant to her, or if she even should at this point, Gail stuffed her hands in her pockets and tried desperately to think of something, anything, that would make him want to come back.

"I won't be gone forever, you know."

Her response came out without thought. "Promise?"

"If it's within my power, I'll be back."

Gail's eyes widened and she stopped to look at him. "Where are you going? And just how risky is it?"

"I can't answer either question. Partly because of the nature of the situation. Partly because I just won't know until I get there. But a car is picking me up in" —he looked at his watch— "about an hour. So there's not much time."

Once back at Gail's second-floor digs, Aidan quickly packed his bag and took a moment to really see what Gail's place was like, something he hadn't taken time to notice last night. Her apartment was a tiny two-bedroom, but she'd furnished it with modern-looking furniture that didn't scream "sci-fi futuristic." Clean lines and soft beiges and charcoals, broken up here and there with splashes of red. He liked it.

He found her in the kitchen making sandwiches.

"I—I didn't know how long you'd be traveling. Tuna is all I have. I don't keep meat around. I wish now that I did. Then I could send you off with a much heartier meal than this. If I had more notice, I could bake you some cookies. I may not cook, but I do bake a mean dessert. I've added some carrots, though." She held up her hand. "And this apple."

She was babbling. And he smiled as he realized why. She was worried. Aidan took the apple from her hands and set it on the counter. Wrapping her in his embrace, he took a deep breath. "It's kind of nice to be worried about."

Gail tucked her head under his chin as he stroked her back. The alpha male protectiveness that once again surged through him caught him off guard. He'd always been able to let the ladies go. Somehow, this one was proving to be a more difficult exit. For the first time in a very long time, he wanted to reassure someone.

"But you can't give me any idea of when you'll be back, right? Or where you're going?"

Aidan had always loved these calls that meant leaving immediately and not telling anyone. This was his way of life and he shouldn't have to feel like he needed to explain himself. Still, this seemed...different. He'd never experienced being worried about. Ever. Deep inside, he felt something melt, just a little. "I'll be back before you know it."

"You will?" Gail sniffed in his shirt.

He cupped her head in his hands, making sure she could see him respond. "As soon as I can." His gaze followed his hand as it caressed her hair. "There's something about you, Gail Grayson, that makes me want to return."

"You do?"

"Yep. Maybe," he said with a twinkle returning to his eye, "I sense a bit of the leprechaun hiding behind those beautiful brown eyes."

He was gratified to see a smile. "After all, we Irish need to stick together, eh?"

When Gail chuckled, Aidan felt the warmth straight through to his soul. He kissed her then. It wasn't the kiss of two people who knew they would soon be in bed together. It was gentle, urgent, worried, and full of promise.

Pappy sat at their feet, his whine offset by the wagging of his tail. Gail looked down at her dog then back at Aidan. "Hey, why isn't he barking at you?"

Aidan shrugged. "Dunno. I guess he figured out I'm a stand-up kind of guy."

The suspicious look in her eyes became more dejected as the doorbell rang, a harbinger of their imminent separation. Aidan set her away from him reluctantly. "In case you were wondering, I don't have a girl in every port."

Her eyes widened.

"This" —he waved to her and back at himself— "is new to me. I don't know what we have here, but I fully intend to come back and find out."

"O-okay. I'd like that."

The doorbell rang again and Aidan planted one last, fleeting kiss on her lips and grabbed the sack of food, raising it in a thank you gesture. He gave a quick salute with his lopsided, cocky grin in place. "See ya' soon, doll."

"I'm counting on it."

He watched her measured smile begin to tremble at the edges.

"You be careful," Gail said as she tapped him on the chest.

Then he was out the door. Before he took two steps away from the closed door, he heard her.

"He found your treats, didn't he, Pappy?"

Aidan nodded his head and chuckled. Halfway down the steps from her second-floor apartment, he stopped. The urge to go back, to pound on the door, and to carry her back to bed, was stronger than he'd thought possible. What for, though? What could he really offer her? Certainly not the lifetime she would eventually want. Aidan had learned a long time ago that relationships weren't meant to be forever commitments.

He handed the driver his bag and slunk down in the back seat for the short ride to the airport. The night lights of San Diego created a twilight that wasn't real, since his watch said it was close to 10:00 p.m. Nightfall was an imposter, just like him. The desire to be with her was like an itch that wouldn't go away. Yet he knew that, if he returned, he would only hurt her.

After she heard his footfalls fade away, Gail laid a hand against the door. "Be safe." What she really wanted to do was rush outside and beg Aidan to stay. Instead, she turned and let the weight of dread in her stomach pull her to the floor. Pappy settled next to her.

Damn it all to hell. It wasn't enough. Why couldn't he have told her something? Anything to help her understand the level of danger he would be in.

She clutched her stomach. *Maybe I don't want to know.*

CHAPTER THREE

The bunker near the Panama Canal that housed their current operations center was dark, having no windows, only bare-bulb light fixtures and desk lamps that cast more shadow than light. With only a handful of men here, it still managed to stink of damp stone and old food. Heat and high humidity amplified the effect.

Maps rolled out on a large table in the center oriented the group to where the issues happened. A whiteboard met the requirements for note taking and triage, but just barely.

Now would be the time for some of those great spy gadgets to show up. Aidan clasped his hands behind his head and yawned, stretching muscles hunched over for way too long. His sweat-stained T-shirt showed how little the one fan in the room actually helped.

He and his partner, Mike Stone, were here because of a new threat. There was almost always a backlog of ships preparing to transit the canal and some were anchored for days off Puerto Amador on the Pacific side of the canal, waiting their turn.

Now, these ships were being hit by some new cell or cells of thieves. And they weren't taking their time. They boarded, grabbed whatever they could, then bam! The pirates disappeared as quickly as they arrived.

"It makes no sense," he said, working the scenario out loud. "There's no rhyme or reason. They aren't going after the same type of ship or even staying in the same area. It seems so random. Where's the pattern?"

He slapped the map table in frustration. Damn. There had to be a pattern somewhere.

"Here's your coffee," Mike said.

The two of them had worked several ops together and had a good working relationship, which surprised a lot of people. Aidan loved a good practical joke, but Mike was all business all the time. Mike's hair was shorter, darker, and cut in a Clark Kent style that made Aidan want to give him a pair of taped-together glasses and a pocket protector. And that's where the real difference between them showed up. Aidan, the jokester, had done exactly that only a few short weeks ago, replacing Mike's wire-rimmed prescription glasses with taped, black magnifying glasses. Mike had rolled his eyes, tossed them in the garbage can, and gone back to work without glasses until Aidan took pity and returned his pair to him. Yep, Mike was all business.

"Coffee?" Mike said again, holding the steaming mug out.

Aidan sniffed, taking the cup. "Whose coffee?"

"Guess," Mike said in a voice edged with sarcasm.

Aidan took a sip and wrinkled his nose. He wasn't sure he could even swallow the vile brew. It wasn't good. Hell, it wasn't even close to good. And certainly wasn't like Gail's coffee. He could picture her now, in her kitchen brewing a pot for him. She didn't even drink the stuff. She drank tea. But she sure could stir up a mean batch of coffee. That wasn't all she could whip up, he thought as he shifted to ease the pressure building against his jeans.

"Yeah, I know," Mike said. "It tastes like it's about the fifth or sixth time those grounds have been used. And don't even ask what they've added to it."

Aidan gulped what was in his mouth and set the cup aside in favor of his bottled water.

"You'd think," Mike said, "being so close to Colombia, they could dredge up a decent cup of brew."

"Yeah," Aidan said, his mind, and his body, still miles away in San Diego. Something Mike said brought him back to the present and he looked at the map.

"What did you say?"

"I said it would be nice if we could get a decent cup of..."

"No, no. Not that. Colombia. You mentioned Colombia." Aidan bent over the map. "We're close to Colombia," he muttered.

Placing one finger on Colombia, he used his others on the spots marking each of the vessels hit by the pirates. He walked over to the board, then back to the map.

"Colonel Rodriguez?"

"Si?" The man who joined them was taller than most men, but carried the stocky build of someone who could wrestle alligators for a living.

Aidan pointed to the location of the first ship. "How long would it take to get from here to here by, say, a small power-boat?" He dragged his finger to the second ship.

The captain leaned over the map. "Maybe, um, eighteen, twenty hours?"

"And when was the second boat attacked?"

"Twenty-two hours after the first one."

Mike Stone grabbed a Sharpie and began to write the pattern on the whiteboard as Aidan drew an imaginary line to the third boat. "And how long to get to this one?"

"Thirty, thirty-one hours, roughly."

"The third ship was attacked thirty-four hours after the second one," Mike said.

"And the fourth one..." Aidan said. "It would take about ten hours to get to this last boat?" He glanced at the captain for his verifying nod. "It was hit twelve hours later."

Aidan slapped the map again. "This is the same crew of thieves doing all of this!"

"It makes no sense, though," Stone said. "There were easier boats, in much closer proximity. Why would they chase all over the place?"

"To keep us guessing. And busy. To throw us off the track of what's *really* going on."

"And that is?" Rodriguez asked, wiping sweat off his bald head with a towel.

"I don't know, damn it. Could be smuggling. Drug trade. Anything." He pointed to Colombia. "We're close enough for it to be drugs. We won't know for certain until we can capture some of them and figure out where they're from."

Aidan turned to the colonel. "Can we put the word out to all ships in the vicinity to be on high vigilance?"

"That notification has already been issued. Panama offered additional patrols, also."

"That's good, but they need to hang back. In order to find out who's behind the attacks, we need to capture at least one of these guys." Aidan yawned again. "All we can do is wait for the next attack. I'm going to crash."

"I'll wake you if anything happens."

Twenty-four hours later, their luck hit. A boarding in progress was thwarted, and all except one of the pirates got away. A Panamanian soldier managed to wing one of the thieves.

Now Aidan and Mike stood on the other side of a one-way mirror in Panama, listening to the local authorities grill the man. There wasn't much they could tell by his appearance. His skin was darker, his hair was coal black, and he'd been mute ever since getting picked up. He had to be in pain from the hurriedly treated gunshot wound, but didn't utter a grunt or groan.

The *policia* were having no effect. Aidan watched the man stare at some spot on the wall as if the officers shouting in his ear weren't even there.

He was not going to budge. At least, not this way. Aidan turned to the colonel. "We need someone who speaks Colombian Spanish dialects."

"There are translators available."

"Good. Bring in a couple, okay?"

They got him on the third try. The door to the interrogation room opened and a man walked in to consult with the officer seated across the table from their prisoner. Aidan remained focused on the pirate as the man spoke to the officer using a local dialect.

It wasn't much, just a slight movement of his head, but his eyes shifted to the person speaking. Their prisoner recognized the local speech.

Aidan and Mike met the translator coming out of the room and had him show them on a map where he grew up. Cali. The center of the fight against drugs.

"From Cali, they most likely truck the drugs to Buenaventura."

Mike nodded as Aidan turned to the colonel. "We believe these boardings are a distraction. The resources of several countries, Colombia included, are centered on these piracy attempts. It makes it much easier for drug runners to leave the harbor when the harbor is barely guarded."

"*Si*. There is good sense in what you say. And the Port of Buenaventura has been a hotbed of activity for years. I suggest some covert scouting to find where they're base in Buenaventura. Then a raid that will hopefully stop this madness."

"It won't stop the drug trade," Mike said.

"No. But it will slow things down for a while. And ships can rest easier as they wait their turn to transit the canal," answered the colonel.

"It sounds like a solid plan. Mind if we tag along?" Aidan asked.

"I would appreciate your assistance greatly."

Two days later, they were ready to move. A warehouse close to the port was their target. Aidan and Mike donned their flack vests and checked weapons. Mike liked the power of a .50 Beowulf semi-automatic and had the strength to use it effectively.

Aidan preferred lighter fare, but just as deadly. He finished checking his MP5 pistol and stretched his neck to relieve pre-raid tension. This part of the job, the waiting, was the part he hated. Anything could happen on an op like this and having time to think about it only magnified the possibilities.

His thoughts drifted back to San Diego as he checked his watch. Gail would be getting up to go to work about now, making herself some tofu concoction for lunch and sipping her herbal tea. Or maybe she was stepping into the shower right this moment. Aidan smiled.

At the tap on his shoulder, Aidan whirled and struck out at the hand. In a matter of seconds, he had Mike's arm twisted behind his back. As soon as he realized who it was, he let go. "Damn, Mike, startling a man about to go into battle isn't smart."

Mike rubbed his shoulder. "Tell me about it. You okay, partner?"

Aidan squirmed as Mike took a good long look at him. "Sure. Why wouldn't I be?"

"I don't know, but this isn't the first time I've caught you daydreaming."

"I wasn't daydreaming."

"Bullshit. You never let anyone near without you knowing it. No one gets that close to you."

The vision hit Aidan almost as hard as the belt raised over him. He clamped a lid on the memory before it took hold. This was no time for reminiscing. "I'm fine."

"Well, you'd better be, because it's go time."

CHAPTER FOUR

Noise permeated the brightly lit workout center like a throng of geese landing lakeside, but Gail tuned it all out. She hit the up button to increase the treadmill's speed, bumping from a casual jog to just shy of an all-out run.

"Careful," Julia said as she walked at a pace on the machine next to Gail that was sedate in comparison. "You'll wear it out."

"Hahaha," Gail panted, but kept right on going. She had some demons to slay. It had been five days with no word from Aidan. Was it really that hard to find a phone? Of course, if he was deep undercover, maybe he was being watched. One slip and...

She took the speed up another notch. Falling for some undercover operative was either going to get her really fit, or kill her.

"Want to come over for dinner tonight? You look like you could use the distraction."

Puff, puff. "Sure." *Puff.* "Distraction...good."

"Great. Bring some old clothes," Julia said.

Gail glanced at Julia. Old clothes? That was a strange request. "Why?" *Puff.*

"Well, since you're going to be there anyway, you might as well help Hawk paint the baby's room. I'm not supposed to go anywhere near the fumes."

The very unladylike guffaw that Gail let loose almost caused her to miss a step. "Crazy." *Puff, puff.* "Friend."

"Yep. That's me. So, still coming over?"

Gail nodded. She'd help paint. But it wouldn't help her forget. She punched the up button and started to run hard. And wondered, for about the thousandth time, what Aidan was doing at that moment.

The raid went like clockwork. Pallet loads of white-powder cocaine were seized, making it likely this would go down in history as the largest drug bust ever. Aidan and Mike had hung back during the primary operation, deferring to Colonel Rodriguez and the local authorities.

Now, with the op pretty much over, Aidan sat on a large crate and watched the men wrap up. Even though these *policia* were from two different countries, it was apparent they had worked together to combat the outsourcing of drugs on many occasions. They were efficient and worked like a well-oiled machine. Aidan was impressed.

The prisoners, with hands tied behind their backs, sat on the floor. Aidan counted seventeen of them and frowned. That many men hanging around an old warehouse should have drawn some attention. Although, considering the fact that this was Colombia, people might have turned a blind eye. Still, it seemed like more men than needed. Aidan watched the group closely.

There. That one. The one whose face was turned to the ground. While all the others cursed their guards, he remained quiet and inconspicuous.

The man knew something. Aidan would bet money on it and he settled back against another crate to watch for the mistake the man would eventually make. He pulled his ball cap low and feigned sleep, schooling himself to be patient.

It didn't take long and the movement was so fast, Aidan almost thought he'd imagined it. But no. The man had looked up. Aidan followed the sight trail to an office that jutted out over the warehouse.

Standing, he took time for a long stretch, then sauntered over to the colonel. "Don't look up," he said. "I think there's still someone in the office. Did your men clear it?"

"*Sí.*" He kept his eyes focused on Aidan. "I sent two of my best men up there. They indicated it was empty."

"Then either they did not look well enough, or you have trouble in your ranks."

"I will go personally."

"If you don't mind, Colonel, I'd like to handle this myself."

The colonel nodded his head in assent.

"Just act natural and give me a few minutes to set up."

"*Si.*"

"Oh, and if all hell breaks loose, send some backup, okay?"

The colonel laughed. "*Si, si.* We do not want to lose so valuable an agent."

Aidan nodded his head at the compliment, then walked around the warehouse, patting guards on the back, smiling and congratulating them on the fine capture. It gave him time to figure a way in. The stairs looked creaky, so he opted for a stack of crates that would get him close enough to an open window to get in.

He asked Mike to position himself by the prisoner who had tipped Aidan off. "Keep him from tipping my hat, okay?"

"I've got your back, man."

On his next pass, Aidan ducked under the overhanging office. Pulling his weapon, he cocked it and tucked it back in the holster to keep his hands free for the ascent.

As he climbed onto the last crate, he heard a shout from below and glanced down in time to see Mike head-butt the prisoner with his rifle, cutting off any further talk.

The cut-off came too late.

Shit.

Aidan heard commotion in the office and made the final leap into the room in time to see two men trying to escape. One was nearly through the outside window, while the other whipped around to face Aidan, gun drawn.

Adrenaline coursed through his body as he reacted. He fired.

At almost the same time, he felt the sting of a bullet creasing his arm.

Aidan's aim was more accurate. The shooter crumpled to the floor. Aidan kicked the gun away and felt the man's throat. His pulse was thready, and Aidan had seen those glassy eyes before. He wouldn't last long.

Aidan whirled as the office door burst open and Mike Stone rushed in. Pointing at the downed man, Aidan jumped through the window, knowing his partner had his back.

The man he chased had already made it down the fire escape and was nearly out of sight.

"*¡Alto!*" Aidan shouted as he aimed his gun.

The man froze near the corner of a building. When he turned back to Aidan, he did it with a slowness that appeared deliberate. Even from this distance, Aidan could see the mixture of grief and fury in his face.

"Le encontraré. Y escupiré en su sepulcro." The man's voice was low but carried across the alley with a chill that would do Vincent Price proud, just before he disappeared from sight.

Aidan's body reacted with a shiver as his mind translated the words.

I will find you. And I will spit on your grave.

A dark, modern sedan pulled into the loading zone outside the open air market and waited. The man in the shadows waited also. Five minutes. Then ten. When he could discern no increased attention on the car, he left the safety of the dark doorway and walked with a confident stride. In what seemed like a perfectly timed ballet, the door opened, he jumped in, and the sedan moved off into traffic.

Carlos Salvena took the towel his aide offered him and held it to his face. *Carlito! Mi hijo!* His whole body shook as the pain of loss surged through him. *My blood. My only son. Dead.*

He gave grief its head for several minutes, then with a long, shuddering breath, he reined it in. He wiped the grimy streaks from his face with one final sniff, then sat tall and resolute, running manicured fingers through the dark hair that brushed the base of his neck.

"Take me to Cali."

"Already en route, sir." The lanky, studious young man who spoke without a single hint of a Colombian accent never looked up from his keyboard.

"And get someone into that warehouse. I do not want my son's body defiled by those vermin. He will have an honorable funeral."

One twitch was the only indication of surprise the aide gave. "Done."

"*Bueno*," he said in a voice that belied his turmoil and pain. "We have much work to do. Someone tipped the authorities. We *will* learn who."

"Yes, sir. What information can you give me to begin the research?"

The world's most formidable drug lord tossed the aide his cell phone. "There is a picture there of the man who killed Carlito." His only son had been killed in this raid that had come out of nowhere and he intended to focus on the only thing he could. Revenge.

"Find out who that is. And quickly."

"Yes, sir. We will find him," his aide said.

Carlos Salvena did not watch the scenery pass by. Instead, he stared into the blackness of the partition that separated him from his driver. Two fingers tapped the arm rest, the only concession he gave to the lingering pain. This was not the time to wallow in grief. It was the time for paybacks. "I will make him pay dearly for what he has cost me."

CHAPTER FIVE

June Gloom had descended on San Diego with its usual quiet touch. A drizzle almost naked to the eye still managed to seep through clothes and chill the skin. This was the month San Diegans stayed indoors.

Gail's mood mirrored the gray world outside. Even Pappy lay on his bedding, staring at her with those soulful eyes of his. She stared at the pile of work she'd brought home, but she simply wasn't in the mood.

She picked up a magazine and flipped through pages without reading them. Her TV was set to some reality show she didn't even watch.

Where are you right now, Aidan? Only one week had passed, but it felt like months.

Damn it! This waiting around for some morsel of news felt like torture. She tossed the magazine aside and got up, pacing to the kitchen and pouring a glass of old Chardonnay.

After a sip that told her she probably should have put the cork back in when she opened it a couple days ago, she dumped the rest of the bottle and flounced back onto her couch. Determined to find something to pass the time, she picked up the remote and flipped through channels looking for anything that would divert her attention. Nothing did.

Getting up, she stood in the middle of the room, trying to remember where she'd been going. Then her phone rang.

"Hello, darlin'."

"Aidan!" The word came out in one big thank-God-you're-okay-I'm-going-to-kill-you whoosh, along with all the air in her lungs.

"In the flesh. Okay, so not exactly in the flesh."

You're safe! Gail's knees went all wobbly and she plopped down on the couch, trying to clear the mist from her eyes. "I'm-I'm glad you're all right."

"No bullet holes this time."

"W-what?"

"Hey, doll. It's okay. I'm all right and never was in any danger. Your voice is shaking," Aidan said. "Are you okay?"

"I am now."

"You were worried about me, huh?"

Gail let her relief bubble up into laughter. "Now why would I be worried about you? You told me you could take care of yourself."

Aidan's voice switched to serious. "I *can* take care of myself. Remember that. You don't ever need to worry about me."

I can't help it.

"Anyhow," Aidan said, the amusement back in his voice, "there's something else I'd rather be taking care of right now."

"And what would that be?" Gail started to twirl the tassel of a couch pillow in her fingers.

"You."

The word echoed down Gail's back and settled at the base of her spine as a restless tingle.

"So, what are you wearing?" Aidan continued.

Gail looked down in horror at the bunny rabbits dotting her comfy old flannel pajamas. Thick socks hid toes that needed a pedicure. "Ummm…"

"Wait! Don't answer that," Aidan said. "Go change. I'll call you back in five."

"Make it ten!" Gail shrieked as she tossed the phone on the couch and bolted for her bedroom.

Twelve minutes later, Gail shut the light off and closed the door on her tornado-ravaged bedroom, settling comfortably on the couch to wait.

Her phone rang and she let a slow, seductive smile spread across her face before she answered. "Your timing is perfect."

"I'm very good at timing," he said.

Gail flashed to his face above hers as he'd moved in rhythm with her. "I remember."

"Shall we try this again?"

"What have you got in mind, lover?" She drew the last word out into a sultry invitation.

"Well, for starters, what *are* you wearing?"

"Hmmm. Well, you remember my sheets, right?"

"You mean those satin ones I kept damn near sliding off of?"

"Yes."

"You're, um, wearing your sheets?"

"No," she said, laughing. "But the pale pink robe I'm wearing is made of the same soft, smooth, silky satin."

A pause and a quiet "oh" was Aidan's only response.

"And the only thing holding this smooth, silky robe together is a little strap of material around my waist." Gail ran the belt strands through her fingers, enjoying the feel of the material she was describing.

"What's underneath?" he asked.

"Wouldn't you like to know?"

"Oh, yeah. I'm picturing you slowly separating the belt and pulling it apart."

"I'm way ahead of you." Gail's fingers moved to untie her belt. She took her time, letting the ends slip through her fingers again. "Now I'm running my hands up the edge of the robe until I reach my neck. The satin feels so cool on my skin."

"Yeah."

Gail leaned her head back on the cushion. "I'm sliding my fingers along my neck, feeling the skin heat beneath my touch."

"Uh huh."

"My fingers trail under the lapel and, bit by bit, I pull it open. Not all the way, mind you. Just enough to see that I've got something sexy on underneath. The robe moves as I do and the silk feels like a feather's touch as it moves across my skin."

Gail's sigh was long, deep, and satisfying. And echoed on the other end of the phone.

"Underneath, I'm wearing a teddy. Would you like me to describe it?"

"Uh huh."

"I run my hands over satin the same color as my robe. Only this is trimmed with bits of lace."

Aidan didn't answer so Gail made sure she had his attention. "*Very* sheer lace," she said. "In *very* strategic places."

She was rewarded with a sharp intake of breath on the other end of the phone.

Gail shifted into a more comfortable position and put the phone on speaker so she could set it down. "Can you still hear me?"

"Oh, yeah," Aidan answered.

"Good. I'm on the couch. The robe hangs off my shoulders and I'm moving my hands down my body, through the valley between my breasts, and down, down, down. Just as I reach the edges of the teddy, my hands begin to climb upward again.

The material caresses my nipples as I move. I circle each tip, but they ache for more. They ache for your touch."

"Touch." The word came out as more of a squeak than a sound and Gail smiled.

"All in good time, lover. I'm sitting up now. I slide the robe off my shoulders, then lie back onto the cushions of my couch. My hands are free to roam now. As I cup my breasts, they beg for more."

She paused.

"And?" Aidan said in a whisper.

"My body is on fire with thoughts of you, Aidan. My hands move over my body, wishing they were your hands. I caress the sides of my body, move onto my thighs, then across my stomach. I feel bare skin dotted with goose bumps, even though it's warm in my apartment. I feel skin because this teddy is open in the front, held together by one itty bitty little tie between my breasts."

Gail remained silent for a long moment as she enjoyed the desire raging through her. She ran her hands along her body again. The need to please herself was overwhelming, but if they were going to do this, she wanted it to be mutually satisfying.

"I arch my back with need, wishing you were here to touch me, to satisfy me in ways no one else can. My fingers caress hard nipples through the lace. I ache for your touch."

A grunt was her only answer.

"Now, ever so slowly, I pull on the tie that holds this little wisp of cloth together." She looked down. "It releases and the fabric falls open about an inch, showing the cleft between my breasts."

Another grunt.

"I run my hand along the cleft. My body moves with an almost overwhelming need, so my other hand wanders again across my stomach. The teddy separates farther and one rosy nipple peeks out."

"Shit." A commotion on the other end of the phone stopped her.

"What's wrong?"

"Nothing," Aidan grunted. "I just fell over something."

"Are you all right?"

"More than all right. You were saying?"

Gail chuckled. "I was about to describe how it feels to pinch my nipples. Sensation shoots to the vee between my legs. I'm so hot, I don't know how much longer I can keep this up."

With her head back in the game, she sighed. "Did I mention that the panties I'm wearing are see-through? My hand settles there, lightly running up and down. Hmmm."

"What?"

"They're, um, damp."

"Oh, my gawd."

She heard some movement on the other end of the phone, then Aidan spoke again.

"Where's—where's your other hand?"

"My other hand moves from nipple to nipple, circling, pinching, caressing. I reluctantly leave my breasts to pull my thong down."

At the quick intake of breath, she smiled. "Oh, didn't I tell you I was wearing a thong?"

"Uh, no."

"Well, it doesn't matter, because I'm not wearing it anymore. Now I can return to my gentle movements. Up, down, around. I touch myself everywhere. My body is on fire. There's just one more thing I need before I can be satisfied."

Gail could hear his raspy breathing on the other end of the phone and paused.

"What's that?" he urged.

"I need you...to tell me I win this round."

A long moment of silence was broken by a guffaw that she could swear she heard echoing off the walls. When he could speak again, he simply said "maybe" then asked her if she was still hot.

"I'm so hot I could burst."

"Want to finish this?"

"More than anything. Damn, but I wish you were here."

The sound of her doorbell made her jump off the couch. "Crap!"

"What's wrong?"

Frantically pulling on her robe, it was Gail's turn to grunt. "Someone's at the damn door."

"Don't answer it."

"I can't do that."

"Well, then, get rid of them quick, okay? I don't think I've ever been this hard. I can't hold out much longer here."

"'Kay. I'll get rid of them in record time." Gail opened the door with more force than necessary and the grinning form of Aidan Walker stood in front of her. "Aidan!"

"Actually," he said, "I think I win."

"Oh, who the hell cares?" She grabbed his T-shirt with both hands and yanked him inside. The door slammed shut and they crashed into it. Hands were everywhere as Aidan took over where she left off and she worked to free his erection. His pants fell down around his ankles as he turned her so her back was up against the door, picked her up, and entered her.

Desire raged through Gail, the same deep need Aidan showed as he thrust in and out, pounding into her. Her fingernails scratched, then dug into his back as they both crossed the threshold and climaxed in one fast, furious, rolling bolt of thunder.

Gail started to shake and had no clue how Aidan still managed to hold her between him and the door. Her body was in total meltdown mode.

Moments later, Aidan let her feet slide to the floor and they leaned against each other to catch their breath.

"Okay," Gail gasped. "You win."

Aidan chuckled. "I think we both won."

CHAPTER SIX

Aidan tossed on shorts and a T-shirt and blinked at the bright light as he entered Gail's kitchen the next morning. He rummaged through the oak cupboards, holding out little hope for actual food, and smiled as he opened the fridge. It was now stocked with eggs, milk, cream and coffee, yogurt and fruit. The meat drawer yielded a rasher of bacon and some ham.

He started a pot of the hair-growing brew he preferred, then prepped a teakettle. Next, he dug around for pots and pans.

By the time Gail joined him, he was into his second cup, munching on bacon, and had an omelet about done. He turned the simmering teakettle back on.

"Wow," she said, combing her hair with her hands. "You can cook."

"I am a man of many talents." He held out his arms and she slid into them as he fingered the edges of her pale pink satin robe. "I think I'll always love this robe."

Gail smiled. "So will I."

The teakettle started its banshee call, so Aidan tapped her on her very delectable bottom. "Get yourself some tea. Breakfast" —he waved his hands at the stove— "will be ready in a sec."

As she settled into a chair at the retro-looking metal table, Gail took a sip of tea and spoke. "I do believe I could get used to having you around, Aidan Walker."

Aidan jerked as "I do" ran through his brain at breakneck speed. In the process of flipping an omelet, he scrambled to land it in the pan.

Gail's trilling chuckle eased the tension in his back as he served up breakfast: one vegetarian omelet and one loaded with meat.

"Don't worry, sexy man. I'm not planning a wedding or anything."

He stifled the shudder that word evoked and tried to play it off with an exaggerated swipe of his brow. "Whew!"

He should have left during the night. That was his rule. You love 'em and leave 'em. What was it about this woman that made him break his cardinal rule? He didn't do morning-afters. They gave him a huge case of the heebie-jeebies and he knew exactly why. People didn't stick around. He'd learned that the long, hard way and had resolved ages ago to leave before that could ever happen.

The problem was, Aidan felt happy here. Now.

He didn't *want* to leave. At least, not as long as they didn't talk about the "m" word. His job, though, wasn't a nine-to-five thing. It was with him all the time. The memory of that threat caused Aidan to frown. Could it follow him here?

He glanced around the kitchen before his eyes settled back on the pixie in pink sitting across from him. Her feet were tucked up underneath her as she dove into the omelet with relish.

"Mmmmmm." She took another bite. "This is so good. I can't believe this all"—she pointed her fork at the food—"came from my kitchen." Gail swallowed and paused. "Ummm, Aidan?"

"Yeah?" He chewed on a piece of bacon.

"We didn't use any protection, you know, that first time last night."

It took him a moment to switch gears. When he did, he froze mid-bite as the food turned to acid in his mouth. In fact, his whole body froze as the bullet of information filtered through his shield to his brain. He'd made sure this very conversation could never happen before. Ever. Always careful. Always certain. No chances taken. Then, one look at Gail and it all flew out the window.

Aidan scrubbed a hand through his hair. The need to be with her had been beyond intense and had seemed so natural, he hadn't given protection a thought. He could feel her gaze on him, but stared at his plate as he tried to formulate a response. Placing his fork on the plate as if it were fine, breakable china, he leaned back in his chair.

"No. We didn't use protection, did we." It was a statement, not a question and he knew his voice was about as flat as it could get. He could tell by the narrowing of Gail's eyes.

"Nope. Got caught up in the moment, I guess."

He shook his head. "What the hell have you done to me?" He'd meant to think the words, but the fire now erupting from her eyes told him he'd said them out loud.

"Me? What did *I* do?" She pushed back from the table and stood, only just missing him as she yanked her plate off the table. "So, I suppose if I get pregnant, that will be my fault, too?"

"No!" He brushed the hair off his face. "It's not just your fault. We *both* forgot. I just...I don't want kids, Gail. I—I won't bring kids into this world."

She turned to him, omelet plate still in her hand. "Why not?"

"The why isn't important. I won't. Have you—?" He stopped and tried to figure out how to pose the question. "Are you—?"

"Had to go off the pill for medical reasons."

"Maybe we should talk to a pharmacist about the morning-after pill?"

He watched her closely as he asked. Her answer was apparent in the flush in her cheeks and the way she opened and closed her mouth several times as she tried to formulate words. She wasn't going to go for it.

When she did speak, the words made his gut spasm.

"Sorry. Not a believer in that." Gail tossed the omelet in the garbage disposal and started stabbing it with her fork to get it to go down.

Aidan didn't try to stop her. He didn't even try to answer her. Fear paralyzed him. Until he looked up and saw the accusatory look in her eyes. It was too much to deal with, and right now, if he spoke, he'd probably say the wrong thing and totally screw up this, whatever it was, thing they had going. That mobilized him. Needing time to think, he stood and, with a mumbled "I've got to get out of here," split for the door, grabbing his sandals on the way out. As it closed behind him, he heard something hit the door and shatter. This was so unfair to her. He knew that. But shit. He just couldn't wrap his head around what he'd done.

He ran down the stairs, threw his shoes on, and struck out at the fastest pace he could. He quickly found himself on the outskirts of Balboa Park and plopped down on a bench. Where the hell was he going?

No protection. How the hell had that happened? He'd *never* lost his cool like that before. Shit. What if she got pregnant?

If she didn't believe in the morning-after pill, there's no way she would believe in anything else other than keeping the baby. Not that he could...oh, hell.

With shaking hands, Aidan pushed his hair back, leaned forward and dropped his elbows onto his knees.

Shit. Shit. Shit.

The park faded, replaced by a food court he had burned into his memory. And the sad eyes of his auburn-haired mother as she set hamburger, fries and a pop in front of him. She'd made him wait while she hugged him, then cupped his face.

"You know I love you, don't you, baby?"

He'd been more interested in the burger than in reassuring his mother, so the only answer she got was a grunt as he stuffed a fry in his mouth.

"I'll always love you, baby. You remember that."

"'Kay." Another French fry disappeared.

"Good. Now..." She'd taken a deep breath and stood up. "I'm going to go take care of some things. You wait right here, okay?"

"Yeah," he'd said with a mouthful of burger.

Then she'd said the strangest thing. "You're going to be okay now, baby. You'll be much better off."

She'd walked off then. He remembered her walking off, all aglow in the sunlight like she was some sort of angel.

He didn't know how many hours passed as he waited. His stomach had started to make that funny hungry sound. Finally, a nice woman bought him another hamburger and asked him where his parents were. He'd told her his daddy was gone, but his mommy was coming back to take him home. She said she was.

She'd promised.

The nice woman had made a couple of phone calls and sat with him until the police arrived. She'd waited with him while they called Child Protective Services.

She'd gone all watery-eyed as he'd been led away by the case worker.

She'd been very nice to him.

He'd been only seven years old.

And he still remembered it like it was yesterday.

Aidan got up and started walking, deeply into his own thoughts. He'd been abandoned, as it turned out, by both his mother and father. When he'd been old enough, he'd gone hunting. His father had spent time in jail before disappearing. Turns out, his mother had run away as a teenager from an abusive home, taking up drugs to forget, and she'd gotten a trip to the morgue for her efforts.

He came from the broken family of a broken family and he damn sure wasn't going to bring a child into that kind of reality.

Aidan looked up. He was in front of Gail's apartment building. Damn. He'd let his own fears get the best of him and she had paid for it. The only thing she was guilty of was getting caught up in the moment. And he was just as guilty. More so, since this was clearly more important to him.

He'd really blown it. And she deserved an apology.

He climbed the stairs with the weight of the world on his shoulders and opened the unlocked door a crack at a time to keep whatever she had thrown against it from making more of a mess.

It was all gone. There was no shattered plate, no food, nothing in front of the door. Dishes rattled in the kitchen. Aidan closed the door quietly and walked around the corner.

Gail was still at the sink, with water running and a towel in her hands. Except she had stopped working and stood there staring at the blank wall in front of the sink. "Decided to come have it out, did you?" she asked without turning.

He gently pulled the towel out of her hands and turned her into his embrace. It almost unmanned him when she clutched him as if her life depended on it.

"I'm sorry," he said.

Gail sniffled, but instead of answering, she tightened her hold on him.

"I handled that badly."

At least that time he got a muffled "Ya' think?" out of her.

He stood there holding her and let the past fade away. For now.

Eventually, she stirred. "Um, I think the sink's about to overflow."

He chuckled and released her. As she turned off the tap, he tried to explain. "I know I reacted badly. But trust me, I am not good father material."

"I don't get that," Gail said, leaning her back against the sink as she looked at him. "I think you'd be a great parent."

His gut clenched. "Nope. Not me. So, let me ask you again. The pill is out, right?"

"Right."

He tightened his lips. It was time to start praying. "Well, maybe it's a moot point."

"Yeah," Gail said. "Maybe I'm not pregnant."

"After all, it was only one night. One time."

The soft smile of memory touched her face. "We used protection the other times."

His smile joined hers. "The *several* other times."

"Uh huh."

He rubbed his hands up and down her arms. "So, we wait and see what happens?"

"That's all we can do."

"And we deal with it as we have to." His hands moved to her shoulders, then his fingers trailed down her collarbone.

"Sounds good," she said, a bit breathier.

He leaned in and smelled her hair, all citrus and spice. "Did you shower?"

"I had some time on my hands."

"Hmmmm." His hands followed the collar of her robe. "Interested in taking another one? I'm in need of a deep cleaning."

Gail laughed. "You are insatiable."

He raised an eyebrow, then headed for the shower, peeling clothes as he went.

When she slipped out of her robe and joined him a few moments later, he went from interested to rock hard and pulled her under the streaming water.

She met his desire, move for move.

"Now who's the insatiable one?" he asked.

And this time, he didn't forget the condom.

CHAPTER SEVEN

Gail didn't like whiners. In fact, she'd been known to take them to task if she caught one hint of that nasally "Whaaaaa" attitude from her friends. She shuddered as she heard the same sound emanating from her own mouth.

"What do you mean, you have to leave?"

They were jogging in Balboa Park in the last dregs of daylight and, between Pappy tugging her forward and Aidan's longer legs, Gail found it tough to keep up. She tried to lengthen her stride and could have sworn Aidan sped up. He was working way too hard to suppress a grin.

"I wasn't supposed to have a layover here," he said. "I'm already a day overdue for debriefing."

"You...don't...get...vacations?" Damn. Now she was out of breath. Didn't this guy *ever* run out of energy?

"Yes, I do. But I just got off an op. I need to report in."

Huff, huff. "By phone?"

Aidan laughed and put a hand on her arm, slowing them to a walk. He took the leash from her and, with a slight tug, had

Pappy walking sedately beside him. "I thought you said you ran?"

"I jog," she answered. "That's a whole lot different than running." She punched him in the arm. "You weren't making it any easier."

He raised his eyebrows in innocence, then grew serious. "I can't call in. Phone reports don't work in my world, since a lot of what I do is confidential. Regretfully, I have to go back to England and do it in person."

"Oh." Gail felt an ache in her heart that had nothing to do with over-exercising. Aidan was going to leave again and go back to his dangerous job. "When will you be back out this way?"

"I don't know." He frowned. "My job isn't a nine-to-five thing. After debriefing, I could get stuck with days or weeks of investigative paperwork. Or I could get sent right back out into the field."

"Yeah. The dangerous field. The one where I can't contact you and vice versa."

"You knew what I did when you met me."

"Yes, I did. I just thought...maybe we'd get a little more time together before the job intruded again."

They walked in silence as twilight started to blend into the darkness of night. "It's getting late," Gail said. We should get back."

"Yeah."

Inside her apartment, Aidan turned Pappy loose and watched the dog lap at his water. "Why don't you come and visit me?"

"What? In London?"

"Sure. Why not? You've got a passport, right? After all, we met in Mexico." He looked like he'd surprised himself with the suggestion, but the idea was gaining ground.

"Yes. But I can't just leave. There's Pappy to think of. And I have a job, you know."

"What?" His eyes crinkled up as his grin widened. "You don't get vacations?"

"Oh, you!" Gail slapped him in the chest. "No fair."

"Hey, they were your words, not mine. And besides, who ever said I played fair?"

Gail didn't take the bait. Her mind was already spinning with possibilities. England? She'd never been. And to be shown the sights by Aidan sounded absolutely perfect. Still, she did have responsibilities here.

"When do you have to leave?"

He brought his arms up as if shielding himself from an imagined blow. "I have to catch the red-eye tonight."

"That's in, like, three hours!" She hit him again.

"As it is, I'll be going into the office with only the sleep I get on the plane. I'll barely get there in time to catch my boss before he heads home for the night. My ass is in the sling if I don't give him all the particulars and soon."

"Your ass is in the sling for leaving, too."

He swatted her rump. "So come for a visit."

"I'll see what I can do."

"Good enough. Now, can I count on you for a ride to the airport?"

"I guess." She felt the tug of separation already.

"Well, since we've got a little time, how about another kind of ride?"

A world-weary Aidan walked into the headquarters of the International Marine Bureau. Bleak walls offset by the occasional bulletin board mirrored how he felt. Bone-tired and ready for his bed. First, though, he needed to soothe his boss's ire.

It was quiet, as most of the workers had gone home already. Aidan's footfalls echoed as he approached the director's office.

"That you, Walker?" the voice boomed. Now that was a sound he knew well. In all the years he'd worked here, that roar had never wavered. And Aidan, along with just about everyone else in the building, wouldn't want it any other way.

Aidan rounded the corner into the office of Charles "Chuck" Ecker, director of the piracy division of the IMB.

And he just about hit the floor as he stared. It had been, what, a couple months since he'd seen him? Director Ecker had been his usual self, with long hair, bushy beard and massive girth at war with an impeccably designed suit and well shined Oxfords.

The suit was the only thing Aidan recognized. The man's hair now sported the standard office cut and his beard had vanished. Still, even that paled next to the fact that the director must have lost fifty pounds. He looked like a shell of his former self.

"Well, what the hell are you gawking at? Get your ass in here."

"Boss?"

"Yeah, yeah. Just sit, okay?"

Aidan grinned and made a pretense of looking behind the director. "Who are you," he said, "and what have you done with the director?"

"Okay, wise guy. You done yet?"

"Almost. What happened? Did you cave to the powers that be? Oh, wait a minute. You *are* one of those powers."

The director's face had turned a few shades darker than his normal red. "Sit down," he boomed.

Now that voice, Aidan remembered. He sat, but nothing was going to remove the wide grin on his face.

"I had some issues," the director said. "Health issues. So I decided to lose some weight."

That wiped the smile off Aidan's face. Health issues? Their division had gone through a lot of attrition lately. Dion Gaetani had jumped ship to become a philanthropist. Aidan understood why. After Dion's partner of ten years had tried to kill him, he'd lost the desire to do undercover work. Still, they were two agents down with a work load that kept climbing. Chuck Ecker was the only thing keeping them afloat. He shifted his operatives to different situations around the world like pieces on a chess board. And, to a man, they all knew unequivocally that he had their back.

The division would not easily weather the loss of Chuck Ecker. More importantly, Aidan would miss his counsel. The man knew how to cut to the chase.

If he was sick... "You okay?"

"Yeah. I am now. Just needed to get back on track. So I had that gastro-crap surgery. Lost fifty-two pounds so far. Hell of a way to do it, though."

"I bet. Hey, I'm glad you're all right."

The director's skin darkened again and he shuffled through papers on his desk. "Yeah, yeah, yeah. Let's get down to business. It's way past supper time and it's the only meal, small though it is, I can enjoy these days."

Gruff was back. Aidan smiled. He knew gruff.

They spent the next hour discussing the op and Aidan's perception of how it turned out.

"You don't think we're done with whoever this drug lord is, do you?" Chuck Ecker asked.

"He's not in custody. And he's pretty damn pissed off. That's a dangerous combination for someone with his power. So yes, I think he will reappear, and that he will create more havoc than ever before."

"Just how good a look at you did the man get?"

Aidan grimaced. "Good enough that he had time to threaten me."

"Do we need to put you in protective custody?"

"No!" Aidan took a deep breath and calmed down. "No," he said again. "I can't imagine he will identify me that easily."

"Just to be safe, though, I'd like you to stay out of the field for a while."

"Not necessary. Besides, you need all the men out there you can get right now."

"I've got a couple new recruits coming out of training. We'll be fine."

"I don't want to sit behind a desk for the next several months."

The director chuckled. "I doubt it will come to that. Let's just take it one day at a time for a while. In the meantime, I do have some stuff here in the office you can catch up on, like your op reports."

Aidan groaned as the director stood, signaling an end to the meeting. They walked out of his office together as Aidan tried one last time. "Shit, boss. You know I'm better in the field than behind a desk."

"Yes, but deskwork goes with the job. And this is the perfect time for you to pay the piper, my boy." His booming laugh as he walked down the hallway sealed Aidan's fate.

God-damned paperwork. The next few weeks looked pretty damn dreary.

Then he remembered the invitation for Gail to come visit. His footsteps picked up in anticipation. Maybe, this wouldn't turn out too badly after all.

"His name is Aidan Walker and he works for the piracy division of the International Marine Bureau," the aide said.

Carlos Salvena turned from his desk to look out the window. Outside, his plantation looked like the holdings of a rich man. Little did anyone know just *how* rich. A large mansion and manicured gardens made up the main part of the villa. The bulk of the estate spread out in fields of grapes and vintner's outbuildings. His "legitimate" business. The part that kept him outwardly honorable. Most likely, no one was fooled. He gazed at the fields with disgust. He hated the country. Taking solace in the modern furnishings of his office, he hit the button that closed his windows to the outside world. Soon, very soon, he would make his move to America and take his place as the head of the cartel there.

First, though, he had to take care of this man, this Aidan Walker. The one who murdered his son. He hung his head for a long moment as the pain stabbed a new thrust of daggers into his heart. When he raised his head, he glared at his aide as he tested the name.

"Walker. Aidan Walker." *I have you, now. And you will pay.* "Where does he live?"

"In London, sir. Near the headquarters for the IMB's main offices."

"Is he there now?"

"No, sir." For the first time, the aide hesitated. A slight tick in the side of his mouth was the only indication he was nervous. "We have not yet been able to ascertain his whereabouts, sir."

Salvena waited. He knew how to command his men and it wasn't always with a heavy fist, although sometimes that was a necessary...and satisfying...way to deal with incompetence. However, Thomas had been with him for two years now. That was about eighteen months longer than any other personal aide. The man was a technology master and information guru, and Carlos knew he would be hard-pressed to find an adequate replacement. He paid the man well enough that he would never look elsewhere for employment, or loosen his lips.

Still, fear went a long way to maintain order in Carlos's organization. There was power in fear. And Carlos Salvena fed on that power. "I am disappointed in you, Thomas."

Carlos was quite satisfied with the deepening of the tick in his aide's cheek.

"You are usually much quicker to obtain the information I need."

"Yes, sir. This man...this man is elusive. It is as if he disappeared from the face of the earth."

Carlos Salvena frowned, something that he knew his people always took as a bad omen.

"I will find him, sir," Thomas said. "Rest assured that I will find him soon."

Carlos nodded. "I know you will." He paused, giving the man time to let the fear wrap tighter around his spine. "So, my friend, what else have you learned? Why did the IMB come after us? Our business is not their domain."

Back on solid ground, Thomas glanced at the pad in his hand. "Correct, sir. However, our smoke screen was right up their alley. They must have somehow tied the piracy attempts to our operation."

"How?"

"I'm sorry, sir." He gulped air. "I do not yet know."

Salvena hit the expensive glass and brushed metal desk with his palms. "That is not good enough."

"No, sir."

"I will have answers."

"Yes, sir," his aide said.

"And soon."

"Working on it, sir."

"Work faster."

His aide nodded and backed out of the office as Carlos turned to stare at the now darkened windows.

"You have cost me dearly, Aidan Walker. And I will make you pay."

CHAPTER EIGHT

After forcing himself to do paperwork until he couldn't see through exhausted eyes, Aidan headed home and let himself into his apartment. Everything looked the same as before. Same dark leather, same pile of mail. He flipped on the gas fireplace to remove some of the chill. Fall had tripped into England early this year and it would take a while for the furnace alone to heat the place to a comfortable level.

The cold wasn't the only thing that felt off. This place was no different from any other place he'd rented. It was nothing but walls, windows, and furniture. A place to flop between missions. Now, something felt like it was missing. And he knew what, or rather, who.

Damn, but that woman had gotten under his skin. Being with her, at her apartment, he'd been more relaxed than any-where else. He grabbed a beer out of the fridge and checked his watch. It was 3:00 p.m. in San Diego. She was probably still at work, but he didn't care. He just wanted to hear her voice, if only for a moment or two.

He picked up his phone and placed the international call, almost hanging up twice. He should find a way to get her out of his head, instead of ingraining her more deeply inside.

"Hullo?"

Gail's sleepy voice filled him with longing.

"Hey, doll. Did I wake you?"

"Aidan! Hi, uh, no. You didn't wake me at all."

He smiled as he heard sheets rustling in the background. Satin made more noise than regular sheets. He could see her now, sitting up in bed, running her free hand through hair spiking out in every direction. He imagined her sleeping, in nothing, on those satin sheets and stifled the urge before things got uncomfortable.

"You sound like you were asleep."

Gail sighed. "You caught me. I came home early and took a catnap. Someone's been keeping me up to late."

"You never complained."

"And I never will with the talents you have," she said. "You know, since I'm in bed already..."

"It's tempting, doll. Very tempting. But the beer in my hand will probably knock me out before we get past first base. You're not the only one who's sleep-deprived."

"Oh." He could hear the disappointment in her voice. "Okay."

"You are a little temptress, and tomorrow, maybe we see if we're as good as we were before with this whole phone sex thing. For now, it sounds like we both need sleep. I'm hoping you'll be here in person soon. Did you talk to Julia about some time off?"

Gail sighed and settled deeper into her pillows, remembering the conversation with her boss. Julia had danced with joy over Gail's request for a couple weeks off, ecstatic that Gail was letting a guy get under her skin. Gail was a little worried that things were going too fast, though. Aidan spun her world out of control and her attraction to him scared her. A lot. "Yes. I can get the time off."

"Good. I'll book your flight. Tomorrow, okay?"

"Wait a minute, buster." Pleased with his apparent need to see her, and soon, Gail couldn't get too mad at his heavy-handed tactics. "First of all, I can make my own reservation. Second, I can't just pick up and leave. It's a critical week at work and I've already taken one day off."

"And spent it very well, let me remind you."

Gail's hand caressed the phone as if it were Aidan. "Definitely. Still, I have a few things to wrap up before I can leave. How about two weeks from today?"

The impatient sigh she heard on the other end of the phone did more for her ego than any compliment he'd given her to date.

"Well, since my boss has me sitting a desk until I catch up on paperwork, that should be fine." Aidan said. "But catch the red-eye the night before if you can. I want you here."

"I agree."

After finishing the phone call, she took a long moment to stretch, then Pappy jumped on the bed, in full "feed me" mode. Gail got up and headed to get them both dinner, her thoughts still lingering on how nice it was to be woke up, even long distance, by Aidan Walker.

Two weeks later, Gail was having trouble concentrating in the staff meeting. Tonight wasn't soon enough to be on the plane. Talking to Aidan on the phone had its benefits. But it was nothing like Aidan in person. Her stomach was tied in knots, waiting to get out of here and on her way to London.

"What do you think, Gail? Will that work?" The suit on the other side of the table asked the question, and Gail stared at him. She had no idea what he was talking about.

Thank goodness for her boss, who stepped in to cover for her. "I'm sure that will work just fine, Scott. Why don't you work up the details and verify feasibility, and let's re-visit this in a couple weeks."

Julia stood, her rounded stomach stylishly encased in a tummy-molding maternity top. "I think that's about it for today. Thanks for coming, everyone."

After they all filed out, Julia sank back down in the chair and kicked off her heels. "I'm not sure my shoes are going to survive this pregnancy. My feet are killing me."

"Maybe it's time to switch to flats," Gail said. She sipped her water. Her stomach was giving her fits today.

They both glanced down at the stylish red heels lying on the floor.

"Never!" Julia laughed.

Gail saw the luminescence of her friend. "You know, pregnancy becomes you. You're happy. And you look healthier than ever."

Rubbing a hand over her belly, Julia agreed with Gail, then frowned. "You, on the other hand, are looking decidedly pale. You all right?"

"I don't feel very well. I think it's just nerves. I've never flown this far before. And what if..." —she clutched her stomach— "what if Aidan is having second thoughts?"

"How often do you call him?"

"Never. He keeps calling me." She smiled. "Every night."

"Then trust me, he's not having second thoughts. Why don't you get out of here? You're already in England mentally anyhow, so you're not much use to me."

"You're right. My concentration is shot." Gail gulped as a spasm of nausea hit her. She rose and, with a mumbled "Excuse me," ran for the bathroom.

Julia put her aching feet up on Gail's vacated chair, relishing the momentary reprieve from propriety. She stared at the door through which her friend had just departed and a smile slowly spread across her face.

She placed both hands on her stomach. "I think, my son, that you will soon have a little playmate to grow up with."

She shook her head and wondered how Gail and Aidan would take the news when they figured it out.

CHAPTER NINE

Gail wished she could wipe the entire flight to Heathrow out of her mind. The airport in San Diego had been an unusually ghastly struggle with security. Aidan had wanted to pick up a first-class ticket for her, but she'd refused. It seemed like too much, like her world was spinning on some crazy axis and she'd needed this decision to be hers.

She'd paid the price. Stuck in a middle seat between a very talkative older woman and a businessman whose laptop took up his tray and half of hers, she'd gotten no sleep. If one wasn't talking, the other had been tapping away on his keyboard. As well, her queasiness hadn't abated, which meant begging the man's pardon on several occasions to rush to facilities not well set up for bending over a toilet.

She waited for pretty much everyone else to get off the plane before reaching for her carry-on in the overhead. At least Aidan wouldn't be at the gate. She felt the flat spot in the back of her head from leaning against an airplane seat for too many hours. She could take a few minutes to freshen up in the ladies room before she went through customs and met him on the other side.

She trudged up the ramp, pulling her wheeled carry-on, one wheel of which had decided to stick in a direction diametrically opposed to the way she wanted to go. Stopping, she leaned over to fix the wheel and a new wave of nausea almost brought her to her knees. She sped up, knowing she needed a bathroom *now*, not later.

"Hey, doll."

She whirled around and there he was. Aidan. So many emotions rushed through her that she couldn't sort them out. A lot of joy, tempered by consternation and a little anger that he was seeing her in this state, all congealed into a wave of dizziness. She crumpled to the ground.

Aidan caught Gail as she fell and carried her over to a row of seats.

An attendant rushed over. "Is she all right? Should we call for aid?" she asked anxiously.

He felt her cheek, glad to learn she had no fever. She was pale, but the flight could cause that. "She's breathing normally. Let's give her a moment and see if she comes around."

The airline employee rubbed her hands together over and over. "Well, if you think we should."

"Let's give her a bit of room, shall we?"

The attendant moved off, but kept a furtive eye on them.

Aidan stroked Gail's face and tried to tamp down his own worry. Had the flight been that rough on her? He should have insisted on first class. She'd never traveled this distance before and wasn't used to it.

Gail's eyes fluttered open.

"Hi, there," he said quietly.

"Wha—where am I?"

"Right now, lying on what must be an uncomfortable set of airport seats at Heathrow."

"Oh, crap. I fainted?"

"Yes."

"Ugh."

She tried to sit up, but Aidan settled a hand lightly on her shoulder. "First things first. How are you feeling?"

"Fine," she said through tight lips.

"Sorry. Not buying that yet."

"Really. I feel much better now. It must have been the flight. I didn't get much sleep."

He helped her to a sitting position and handed her a water bottle. "Dizzy?"

"A bit. I just need a moment."

"Drink some water. And no rush. We've got all the time in the world." He smiled.

She ran a hand over her hair. "I look like hell."

"You look like you've just spent a bunch of hours either in airports or on planes. And," —he placed a kiss on her forehead— "I think you look great."

"You lie, then." But the smile she gave him was bolder this time.

"Think you can walk? We've made a bit of a scene and should probably get you through customs and out of this place."

"Sure. Hey, how did you manage to be at the gate of an international flight?"

He pulled out his badge. "I've never used my badge for personal gain before. It's kind of a heady power."

He could tell she felt much stronger, but he grabbed her carry-on and insisted she hold his arm as they walked. It felt good to have her beside him.

After a stop in the restroom, he gathered her luggage and stayed with her through customs. They were soon out of Heathrow and on their way to his flat near Southwark Park.

He'd planned to point things out to her during the drive, like Hyde Park and Westminster Cathedral; however, Gail fell asleep before they'd gotten out of the airport parking lot, so sight-seeing, even from the car, would have to wait for another day.

He got lucky and found a parking spot only a few cars down from the door to his apartment.

"Wake up, sleepyhead. We're here."

He had to nudge her a couple times and, even then, he left her luggage and carried her into the building and his bedroom, thanking the gods that his flat was on the first floor. She was a pixie, but even pixies could make stairs seem like mountains.

Gail mumbled some useless words as he got her to drink a little more water, then laid her on the bed and covered her. She drifted right back to sleep, so Aidan brought in her luggage. An hour later, she was still asleep, so he got himself something to eat. He watched television for a while. Hell, he even unpacked her bags, quickly finding out that she did not believe in packing light.

At the door to his bedroom, he watched her even breathing. It looked like she was out for the night. The sleep would do her good, he thought, before resigning himself to another night of celibacy. He tried to sleep in bed next to her, but got so hard just watching her that he gave up and went to crash on the couch.

In fact, Aidan spent the next twenty hours waiting for her to wake up. By lunch the next day, he'd about decided to call the aide car when she finally stumbled out of the bedroom.

Sluggish didn't even begin to describe how Gail felt. The world was a fog and she'd only been partially successful at lifting it.

Aidan's smile tore the fog-sheet a little further.

"Hey, doll." As he rose from the dining table, she could see he'd been working. His laptop was surrounded by littered papers.

"Uh, hi," she said, trying unsuccessfully to rub sleep from her eyes and walk at the same time. She stumbled right into his arms.

"Now this is what I've been waiting for," he said, giving her a quick peck on the forehead.

"Really? You've been waiting for a half-dead zombie with bad breath?"

Aidan laughed and it sounded like the laughter of relief. "Now that you put it that way..."

She ineffectively swatted at his arm.

"Hey, let me finish. Now that you put it that way...yes. I've been waiting for you. In any shape or form, you're the best thing these eyes have seen in a long time."

The warmth that infused Gail went a long way to alleviate her discomfort. She touched Aidan's face. "You look tired."

"I may have been up a few times checking on you."

"Ah. I'm sorry."

"I'm not. I'm glad you're here. And even happier now that you're awake."

She snuggled deeper into his arms and sighed. "Me, too." Her stomach chose that moment to let out a raunchy growl.

They both laughed.

"Good Lord, woman. I think the windows just rattled," Aidan said. "I guess it's your turn to require sustenance, eh?"

Her stomach still felt a little queasy from the flight, but Gail thought she might be able to eat. And she certainly wanted to.

"I kept it simple for today and picked up some muffins."

"Any tea?"

"This is England, doll. Of course we've got tea."

Gail disappeared into the bathroom, surprised to find her toothbrush in the cup next to his on the windowsill. The size of the room also got her attention. She almost had to step into the tub to close the door behind her, and the pedestal sink edged over into the tub's space. Thank goodness there was a shelving unit over the toilet or there would be no room for makeup or...or anything. She did a tight circle, wondering how she would manage in this tiny space.

"How in the hell am I supposed to get ready in a mi-cro-room, for crying out loud?" She thought she'd grumbled the words to herself, but Aidan answered her.

"Uh, the bathroom's a bit small," he said through the door.

"I noticed," she said. "Don't open the door or you'll kick me into the tub."

His chuckle warmed the irritation right out of her.

Minutes later she sat at the kitchen table sniffing the steam off a hot cup of tea. It smelled like heaven and tasted that way, too. As her stomach grumbles subsided, she sipped tea and ate bits of her muffin.

"So," Aidan said, "what would you like to do with what's left of the day?"

She glanced outside at the gloomy London skies. "Well, I had hoped to see some sights, but..."

"I think, since it's already mid-afternoon, maybe today should be a veg day. I tell you what. Why don't you hop in the shower and see how you feel afterward? I've never seen a flight zonk someone out as much as it did you. We should probably take it easy to start out."

"Sounds like a plan my body will appreciate."

Aidan gave her a peck on the nose. "I can think of other things for you to appreciate."

"Down, tiger. Let me get my land legs solidly underneath me first, okay?"

"Definitely."

"Still," Gail said as she set her dishes in the sink and sat on Aidan's lap, "it's something to look forward to."

She kissed his forehead, his cheek, and then his lips, taking time to enjoy the sensations that coursed through her body. By the way he squirmed underneath her, she knew he was barely keeping himself in check.

Moments later, Gail stepped under the hot spray of the shower and her entire body sighed. Muscles she hadn't known were tight began to unwind and she took a couple of long minutes to just stand there and let the warmth wake her sluggish body.

"Need any help?" The shower curtain began to move as a head popped in. "I'd be happy to wash your back. And a few other places, if you like." The gleam in his eyes verified there was a lot more he'd like to do.

Gail pushed his head back out of the shower. "Not this time, lover. I can handle things just fine."

"Okay," he said. "But don't hesitate to call if you need any help."

"I will."

"And I mean, *any* help."

"I've got it." She shook her head and reached for her shampoo, sitting next to his.

An hour later, she left the bedroom refreshed and feeling more herself than she had in days. Her energy level was up and her stomach was under control. A glance at the window showed some late afternoon sunshine had replaced the London gloom. Maybe they could do a little sightseeing after all.

Then she found Aidan on the couch, fast asleep. She crouched down beside him and moved a lock of hair out of his eyes. The man never stirred, which lent credence to the belief that he had done more than just check on her occasionally overnight.

Hungry again, Gail rummaged through the fridge and made herself a salad. Then, she searched the bookcase until she found a good mystery. Grabbing a couple of blankets, she covered Aidan with one and pulled the other snugly around her body, settling into the overstuffed chair to read.

Three hours and one hundred pages later, Aidan stirred. Gail watched as he stretched, at least as much as the couch would let him. Then he opened one eye at a time. When he saw her, his lips quirked up.

"It seems like one of us keeps falling asleep. Great way to start a vacation, eh?"

She laughed. "I'm happy to be here, no matter what we're doing."

"I second that thought." Aidan bounced off the couch and glanced at the clock. "Hungry?"

"I think I could eat," Gail answered, unwrapping herself and stepping into his arms.

"Well, it's too late to wander far, but how about a little local dinner?"

She nuzzled his neck. "Dinner out could be nice." Peppering kisses along the skin at the edge of his T-shirt, she offered another option. "Dinner in could be even nicer."

Aidan growled then, and it had nothing to do with his stomach. Gail pulled his lips down to hers in a kiss that started out as "hello" and quickly moved to a devouring hunger.

Her hands snaked beneath his shirt as she opened her mouth to him and their tongues danced. All it seemed to take with this man was a single kiss and she melted in his arms. And absence seemed to have enhanced the feeling.

Aidan's hands moved through her hair as he tasted her. Earl Grey with a touch of honey. She tasted like, well, like the only place he wanted to be.

He reached down and pulled her hips against him so she could feel his rock-hard need. Her legs wobbled and he pulled back, smiling.

"Made you go all weak in the knees, eh?"

"No way," she countered. "It's jet lag."

He swung her up in his arms and headed for the bedroom. "Jet lag, huh? We'll see about that."

CHAPTER TEN

The next morning, Gail awoke to the smell of eggs and bacon. She stretched in bed, remembering the long night of love-making with little sleep.

And no dinner. Her stomach growled and she took a deep whiff, thinking meat didn't smell so bad after all. Then another sensation worked its way to her brain. She covered her mouth and ran for the bathroom.

Several minutes, and swishes of mouthwash, later, she joined Aidan in the kitchen.

"Mornin', doll. I thought I heard you get up." He pulled her into his arms and took time away from cooking to remind her why she had hopped on a plane and flown halfway across the world. Gail relaxed into him. Oh, yeah. She could definitely get used to this.

"Hungry?"

Thinking of her sudden nausea, she opted to take the safer route. "Maybe just some tea to start out the day."

"You don't eat enough to keep a bird alive."

"I'm just not much of a morning eater, I guess."

"Well, I am." And he proceeded to prove it, piling his plate high with scrambled eggs and bacon. As a piece of bacon fell to the floor, they both called for Pappy at the same time.

"I miss him already," Gail said.

"I don't."

"Yes, you do."

"That dog of yours bit me!"

"It was a love bite. Besides, he loves you now."

"Hmmmm. What'd you do with the little monster while you're here?"

"I used the friend card. And I think it's going to cost me big time in babysitting, because Julia is not really a dog person."

"I can just picture Pappy chasing around that lovely, light-colored house, leaving his gray hairs everywhere."

Gail laughed. "Schnauzers don't shed. Much. Okay, so, Julia wasn't thrilled, even though I have Pappy's daycare picking him up every day. The only reason she said yes was because I threatened to cancel the trip. For some reason, she's ecstatic that I've come to England to visit you."

Aidan mumbled a thank you to Julia, then dove into his food with gusto.

Gail pulled a yogurt out of the fridge, thinking it might settle her stomach. Between that and the tea, she did feel better, but this nausea was starting to concern her.

"Where would you like to go today?"

"Anywhere you are," she answered.

"Want to play tourist, or blend in?"

"Seeing as it's my first time in London, I'll pick tourist."

"Good choice."

Hours later, Gail wasn't so sure. Aidan had called a cabbie friend of his who'd toured them everywhere. Buckingham Palace, where they watched the changing of the guard. The Thames, The London Eye, St. Bride's Church, designed by Christopher Wren and the forerunner of the wedding cake, along with The Tower of London, where Ann Boleyn had been beheaded. Temple Square, St. Paul's Cathedral, and a plethora of other places flooded Gail's mind to overflowing. They had stopped for traditional fish and chips, but she'd only picked at her food. When Aidan frowned, she'd suffered through a piece of her fish. And had ended up in the bathroom shortly thereafter.

Now, as they waited for their guide to pick them up, Gail sat and tried to quell her roiling stomach to no avail. Aidan stood behind her and rubbed her arms sympathetically.

"I don't know what's the matter. Maybe I picked up some sort of bug on the plane." She looked up at him, knowing the sheen in her eyes was very close to spilling over. "I'm sorry, Aidan. This isn't how I planned to spend our time together. I just don't know what's wrong."

"It could be a bug. Or just jet lag. It's only been two days and everyone reacts differently to travel." He leaned down and encircled her with his arms. "I hate to see you this miserable and not be able to do anything."

"I couldn't be miserable." Her smile was weak. "I'm with you."

"Maybe not miserable, but definitely exhausted." He crouched down in front of her. "I'm sorry, doll. We should have taken it easy today."

"No." She rubbed the hand that rested on her arm. "I loved seeing it all."

A honk signaled their ride had arrived. Aidan pulled Gail up and let her lean against him. "Now it's time for you to rest. We're heading home."

"I like that idea."

As soon as he said the word, Aidan broke out in a cold sweat. Home was not a word that brought happy memories to mind for him.

"Home. That sounds nice," Gail said.

The urge to run raced through Aidan's body like a bolt of lightning and he pulled away from the embrace so she would not feel his reaction.

Gail frowned but didn't say anything.

Back at his flat, Aidan settled Gail on the couch, snugly wrapped in a blanket, while he steeped some tea for her. He was glad for the excuse. It gave him time to clear his head. *Home.* The word echoed through his mind. It was like a foreign language whose meaning was just out of his reach. In an instant, he was that frightened little boy who kept insisting he had a home and his mother would be back to take him there.

He grabbed a beer from the fridge and joined Gail, placing her tea near her. After he settled on the end of the couch, he pulled her feet onto his lap. "Your feet are freezing!" He began to rub them and Gail sighed in apparent contentment.

He almost got away with it.

"Why don't you believe in home, Aidan?"

His body froze as indecision filled his mind with all the possible answers, from flippant to serious. He resumed rubbing her feet, opting to stall for time. "What makes you think that?"

"Oh, pul-lease. You acted as if you'd been burned when I said I liked that word. And you've been jumpy and quiet ever since." She wiggled her toes and he realized he'd gripped them too tightly. As he eased off, she continued.

"I might not know your past, Aidan, but I know you well enough that reactions like that scare the crap out of me. So I'm asking for you to explain what memory helped you decide there was no such thing as home."

"I don't think this is the best time—"

"I do."

Damn. The woman just did not know when to let things alone. "Look, it's no big deal," he said.

Gail picked up her tea and took a sip without saying a word.

"Really. It isn't."

At that, she raised her pretty little eyebrow.

"I don't like talking about myself."

"At all," Gail said. "I know more about your friend Dion than I know about you."

"It's nobody's business."

Gail's jaw gnashed back and forth as if a brassy retort was fighting for release. She clamped her lips shut and Aidan swore he could see her counting. When she finally spoke, he was surprised at how calm and relaxed she sounded.

"If we have any shot at a relationship," she said, "then we need to be able to talk about our pasts."

Relationship? Oh, this conversation was going from worse to downright rotten, and quick. He didn't do relationships. At all. Shit. He was in way over his head here. Aidan got up and paced the living room, then sat on the floor in front of her with a resigned sigh. And gave in, not completely sure why he did so. Maybe it was just time.

He told her the story of that seven-year-old boy who'd been so sure his mother would be back. How he'd struggled and cried as they pulled him away from the food court. How he'd scratched at the back window of the car, crying about how his mother wouldn't be able to find him.

Gail listened, aghast at what Aidan had lived through. Despite the casual monotone of his voice, the details he gave validated that this incident was seared in his memory. She wanted to hug him, to make the memories fade, but he shrugged her off. He ran his hands through his hair and stared at the fireplace. So Gail waited until he was ready to continue.

"I ran away from my foster home three times in the next month. They found me at that mall each time. I don't even know how I got there. Finally, they moved me to a different town. That's when, even at that young age, I recognized the meaning of futility."

The idea of that little boy's pain tore Gail's heart out. And the fact that the man was not immune to the ripples from his past glared at her like a neon sign. She clutched her teacup to keep from wrapping her arms around Aidan because she knew he didn't want that. She chose, instead, to nudge him forward. "So you grew up in foster homes?"

"Hmmm. Not exactly. I grew up when I realized how fickle love is. As for the system...I survived it."

Love is fickle? Ouch. Just starting to realize the uphill battle this relationship would be, Gail squelched the thought. The fact that Aidan was even telling her this was a huge leap forward for them. And what a story. Her heart ached for the little boy who'd had to grow up so quickly. "Was foster care rough?"

Aidan shrugged. "Some of the homes were nice."

"And others?"

"Not as much. The last one...well, I was sixteen by then and was pretty much done letting others dictate my life. So I took off. I've been on my own ever since."

"Aidan—"

He stood abruptly, holding up a hand to stop her. It was the first time she'd gotten a good look at him since he started talking and Gail caught a glimpse of just how good an agent he was. His face was devoid of any sense of emotion. It was as if he'd flipped the switch on everything that made him feel.

His next words elicited a different expression from her as he turned to look out the window.

"Understand something. I don't need or want any pity and I don't bemoan my fate. I had a better life than some and not so good as others. I'm telling you this because you were correct.

You do have a right to know why I don't think in terms of home and…and relationships."

The words felt like a slap in Gail's face. First, it stung. She set the teacup down with defined accuracy as her cheeks warmed. Then teeny-tiny needles started to drive themselves in through her skin and straight to her nerve endings. She felt tears starting to form and willed them to die. But pain and disbelief mingled until they hit a critical mass and exploded. She threw off the blanket and stood, hands clenched in front of her like she was ready to throw a punch. God knows, she wanted to hit some-thing. Anything. This was like waking up to find her father, and all of his possessions, gone…all over again. It hurt like the night she found out about her husband, also a leaver. She drew in a long, shaky breath and spoke with the forced calm of a barely simmered anger. "If you don't believe in relationships, then why the hell are you dating me?"

"I—I don't know."

"So, what? You decided it was time to test the relationship waters and I was the patsy you found to help out?"

He turned to her then, a deep frown on his face. "No. It wasn't like that at all."

"Well, what is it like, Aidan? Because I'm a little confused. You came on to me, *not* vice versa. *You* came to visit me in San Diego. *You* invited me to England. How can you stand in front of me now and say you don't want a relationship?"

He shook his head and shrugged. "I wish like hell I had an answer. All I know is that I can't seem to stay away from you."

"Bullshit. You're just like all the men in my life. Love 'em and leave 'em. Isn't that the saying?" She walked over and pounded his chest with her finger. "I've got news for you, Aidan Walker. I'm one hell of a catch. If you can't see that, then you have no business being in my life. Period. If you can't commit, right here, right now, to giving the whole relationship thing a try, then I'm out of here. I *dare* you to try."

She stood there with her chest heaving after her speech, and fear began to override every other instinct in her. Fear that he wouldn't accept the challenge. Words she was desperate to take back hung between them.

Aidan didn't say a word.

"You're just like William," Gail mumbled as she turned to the bedroom. She disappeared inside before newly reformed tears spilled. Slamming the cantankerous old door, it refused to latch and rebounded against the wall.

"Oooooohhhhhhh!" She grabbed the door and put her weight behind it until it stayed closed.

With no other action available as a release, tears fell unchecked and Gail crumpled to the bed. Crawling up to the pillow, she pulled the quilt over her. Aidan's smell permeated everything, making the tears fall harder.

What was the matter with her? She didn't cry. Ever. Why had she ever let this man get under her skin? She clutched her stomach as a wave of nausea hit her and slowly subsided. This didn't feel like some bug she'd picked up on the plane. She thought back to the week before and realized she'd been sick before she'd even gone to the airport. What kind of flu lasted this long?

Gail's eyes flew open and she clutched the quilt to her mouth to keep from crying out. Could it be? Could she be...

She rocked back and forth as reality whacked her in the face. Long, slow hours passed before she drifted into a restless sleep. Hours where no resolution came, only a rehashing of all the issues in her life. What the hell was she going to do?

Aidan stared at the bedroom door. How had this day deteriorated to a knock-down, drag-out battle? And why had Gail, a woman he'd bet had never backed down from a fight, just walked away? He winced at the recalled slamming door, not once, but twice. She hadn't exactly gone quietly.

Sinking down on the couch, Aidan flipped hair out of his face and realized his hand was shaking. Hell, he'd been in much more dangerous situations than this and he'd never gotten the shakes.

He stood and walked to the bedroom door, intent on talking to Gail, then paused. Maybe they both needed to calm down before they could figure this out. And he needed to understand what was happening a whole lot better than he did now. His no-relationship mantra had run smack dab into a little pixie with spiky hair and luminescent eyes. And it scared him worse than any op he'd ever been on.

What the hell had this woman done to him? Aidan placed a hand on either side of the closed door, hanging his head as he wondered what he was going to do about it.

Then his head snapped up. Who the hell was William?

He grabbed the throw and prepared to spend yet another night on the couch, still fuming over some guy he didn't know.

This sure as hell wasn't the visit he'd planned on.

CHAPTER ELEVEN

Daylight filtered in through the curtains as Aidan heard the quiet creak of his bedroom door. After a night spent digging around for a comfortable position and very little sleep, a foul mood had settled over him while he waited for Gail to wake up. Now, though, he realized how much he wanted to see her leaning over him.

He kept his eyes closed and waited for her to come to him. Instead, his eyes flew open as he heard the apartment door.

She was leaving him. Correction—she was gone.

He tossed on jeans and a shirt and headed out without bothering to grab shoes. Aidan hit the street just in time to see her disappear into the corner store. An overwhelming relief flooded through him and he leaned against the building until he could catch his breath.

Last night, he'd fought against it, but right now, in this moment, he knew. The wall he'd put firmly in place so long ago was crumbling. Hell, it was disintegrating, and fast.

Aidan Walker was falling in love with a pixie.

He didn't have time to deal with the ramifications of that reality as the store's door began to swing out. Rushing back inside his apartment, he lay back down on the couch and yanked the cover over him. He closed his eyes and let years of practice still his breathing to a normal pace just as she walked in the door. He wasn't sure why, but he felt the need to give her some time this morning. Himself, too. They had more talking to do and Aidan still wasn't sure what he would say.

Her footsteps stopped for a moment and it took everything he had to not look at her. When he heard her move across to the bathroom and shut the door behind her, he sat up, wondering once again how they were going to finish last night's discussion. There were still too many questions he hadn't answered in his own mind.

Sitting here wide awake and stewing wasn't helping, so Aidan got up and headed for the kitchen.

Gail needed answers. After a sleepless night trying hard to subdue the suspicion that wouldn't let loose of her mind, she'd decided to find out for certain. Her hands shook as she opened the box. Instructions fell out first and she read them, followed them, then waited for the results.

Gail sat on the toilet and clutched her stomach, willing the nausea to abate. Willing the test to be negative. Praying for more time to work things out with Aidan before they had to discuss *this*.

She looked at her watch again. It was time.

She stood and leaned over the sink to the small wand, its plus or minus sign holding her happiness hostage.

Her mouth dropped open when she saw the results.

Positive.

She was pregnant with Aidan's child.

She covered her mouth as she wondered how he would take the news. What he would do. Her nausea was supplanted by a deep ache that grew to monumental proportions at the thought that he would ship her home and be done with her. Blood congealed in her veins and Gail started to shake as a cold that had nothing to do with the temperature descended on the bathroom.

By the time Gail emerged from the bathroom, Aidan had managed to get coffee and tea going, as well as setting some things out to eat. They needed to finish this talk—well, argument really—and breakfast was as good a time as any.

Gail walked into the kitchen looking decidedly pale, and Aidan felt like a heel for what he'd put her through last night.

"Come on and sit down, doll. Your tea's just about ready." He said the words quietly and smiled to lighten the mood, but she didn't react at all, other than a mumbled "thanks."

That worried him more than anything. Last night wasn't irreparable. They could talk this out and get past it. He was sure of it.

Then he remembered the name and scowled.

"Who the hell is William?"

Gail's head rose like a whip and she glared at him, a mask of defiance firmly lodged on her face. For a long moment, he wondered if she would even answer him.

"William was my husband."

"Your—" It was Aidan's turn to stare as the words filtered through the shock and settled in the part of his brain reserved for things he chose not to believe. "You...were married?"

"Yep."

This defiance thing of hers had worn a hole in an already thin veneer of patience. "And you didn't think to tell me this before now?" He tossed the kitchen towel on the table. "Nice. You give me crap for not opening up to you, then you drop this bombshell on me."

"Unlike your past, mine doesn't affect our relationship."

He moved in until they were face-to-face and said the word with quiet exaggeration. "Bullshit." Backing up, he continued. "You told me last night I was just like him. So that whole he-doesn't-matter thing? It doesn't fly. How long were you married?"

"Two years."

"And?"

"And what?"

He ground his teeth together. "And what happened?"

"He left me."

This time, Aidan played her game and kept silent. It took several moments, but she spoke again.

"For another woman." She glared at him. "As he walked out the door, he apologized and said he was sorry. That he just wasn't the marrying kind. Just like you."

"Wait a minute. You can't lump me in with that asshole just because I said I don't believe in relationships," Aidan said.

At that point, the tough-girl façade crumbled and Gail put her face in her hands. "It doesn't matter now, anyhow," she cried.

Tough, he could handle. But this, this weeping thing? This was not the Gail he knew and he had no clue how to deal with her. He dropped down in front of her and pulled her into his arms.

"Ah, I'm sorry, doll. I didn't mean to make you cry."

"It's not you. It's—" She clamped her mouth shut.

"What?" Aidan nudged her chin up and his heart broke at the tears in her eyes.

"I went down to the corner store this morning."

"Yeah," he admitted. "I saw you leave."

"Well, you didn't see the bag I returned with. I—I picked up a pregnancy test."

Aidan froze as bile climbed its way into his throat and lodged there, making it hard to breathe. Only his time undercover kept him from tensing and backing away. Still, Gail must have sensed his turmoil because she stiffened in his arms.

He released her and stood, backing up to lean against the kitchen counter. He couldn't quite bring himself to ask the question. Each time he tried, his throat turned desert dry.

He gulped twice before he could finally speak. "So," he said, "is it positive?"

It was Gail's turn to lose her ability to talk. This was it. This was where the relationship they apparently didn't have would fall apart. She felt it in her soul and it muted her voice. All she could do was nod. And pray.

Aidan expelled air through tight lips as his chin hit his chest. When he lifted his head, his laughing green eyes had become unreadable.

Gail wanted to run to him, wrap her arms around him, beg him to tell her everything would be all right. Instead, she sat there, her bare feet not feeling the chill of the tile floor. Since Aidan seemed unable to move, she wrapped her arms tightly around herself for the solace Aidan quite obviously couldn't bring himself to give her.

He opened his mouth to speak, then shut it again. Without saying a word, he turned and walked out of the kitchen.

Gail crumpled as the wave of Aidan's reaction washed over her. He didn't want this child. Hell, he didn't want any child. *Oh, baby, I'm so sorry.* Still holding her stomach, Gail straightened as the realization hit her. She wasn't apologizing to Aidan, but to the unborn child she carried.

Aidan may not want this child, but she did.

Even if that means... Gail held tightly to the table to keep from swaying. *Even if that means Aidan can't be part of our lives.*

She went to find Aidan, but he was gone. Sinking down onto the couch, she pulled the throw around her shoulders and rocked back and forth, trying to think of a way to convince him they could make this work.

When he returned an hour later, she was both calm and dressed. "That was pretty chicken-shit of you."

Aidan grimaced. "Yeah, it was."

"You ready to talk about this now?"

"I'm..." He scrubbed his chin. "What are you going to do?" Aidan asked without preamble.

"About what?"

"About the baby." He glanced at her, then stared at the floor.

"Aidan, we've only just found out. I think we both need time to let it sink in before we can decide anything."

"I don't." The chill in his voice fed the cold seeping into her soul.

The heavy feeling returned to her stomach. "What exactly does that mean?"

"I told you before. I never wanted to bring a child into this world. I can't raise a child."

"Well, it's a little late for that."

He took a deep breath and turned to stare at her. "No, it's not."

"What, do you expect me to have an abortion?"

"No!" Aidan shook his head.

"What, then? Adoption?" Now her voice went cold. "I won't give our baby away."

Shaky hands raked through hair she'd run her own hands through only a few short hours before. Aidan took a deep breath and turned eyes to her that finally showed some emotion. They showed a tormented soul.

"I can't be a father, Gail."

"Why not?"

"I thought I explained this last night. I'm just not good parent-material. My genes aren't skewed that way."

"Don't you think, if you gave yourself some time to get used to the idea—"

"No." He moved to her side and spoke quietly. "Trust me, doll. You don't want me to step into this role."

Afraid of the answer, Gail played her trump card. "You don't have much of a choice."

"Actually, I do."

She nodded her head slowly. "I see." She left him and went into the bedroom. Staring at the bed where they had made such tender love, she couldn't be there. In the bathroom, she sat on the side of the tub, her knees knocking against the toilet, as she tried to think. Tears dripped in sad lines down her face.

Before long, she heard the front door close and knew he was gone again. With a sigh that held depths of physical and emotional exhaustion, she got up and reached for her suitcase.

An hour later, Aidan still had not come home and Gail slipped into a cab without another word having been said between them.

CHAPTER TWELVE

"We've found him," the aide said.

"Where?"

"In London. And he has a woman with him." Thomas shielded the Bluetooth in his ear and stared off into space for a moment. Turning his attention back to Carlos Salvena, he continued. "She appears to be leaving. A taxi just pulled up and she has a suitcase with her."

Carlos Salvena smiled then, letting the satisfaction soak in and permeate his mood. He stood and clapped his aide on the back. "This is good news, Thomas. Very good news. Now, here's what you must do..."

Gail took one last look at the window to Aidan's world while the cabbie stowed her case. Then she climbed in, knowing she turned away from the man she'd fallen in love with. But he didn't love her back, at least not enough to find a way for this baby to be a happy thing between them. Gail settled a hand over her stomach and refused to look back as they pulled away.

She didn't see the sedan following them all the way to Heathrow. Nor did she see the man follow her into the terminal and up to the counter. She gave the woman her name, bought a ticket, checked her luggage, and turned around.

The man she hadn't seen was no longer there.

Aidan knew the house was empty as soon as he opened the door.

Damn.

He stood in the entryway. His legs seemed frozen in place and wouldn't accept his commands. Of course, his heart didn't feel much like giving commands. It felt...as empty as his apartment.

He forced himself inside and shut the door. In the kitchen, he automatically poured himself a cup of coffee.

It cooled on the counter without ever being touched. Instead, he reached in the cupboard for the bottle of single malt he kept for occasions that warranted it. Sloshing some into a glass, he toasted the bottle.

"I'd say recent events count."

Hours later, or maybe it was days, the pure torture going on in Aidan's head woke him. The blood in his brain pounded out a beat to the tune of a thousand cymbals. They were joined by the shrill intonation of a trumpet at high pitch.

Aidan sat up and the crescendo grew more insistent, making him dizzy with its siren song.

Then the trumpet sound separated itself from the rest. It wasn't actually a trumpet. It was his door buzzer. And it was getting insistent.

"I'm coming!" He clutched his head when the sound of his own words impaled his brain to the back side of his skull. "Someone shoot me and put me out of my misery," he grumbled.

Throwing open the door, he was shocked to see an old friend standing there. "Dion?"

"Ah, damn. My covert skills must be getting rusty. You saw right through my disguise."

Aidan opened the door farther to let his friend, Dion Gaetani, into the apartment. "What the hell are you doing here?"

"I'm in town to meet with Harrods about a charity event they're sponsoring, so I thought I'd stop by." He clapped Aidan on the back, which set the bells in his head clanging again.

Aidan's voice was much quieter as he responded. "It's good to see you, man. How's Claire?"

"Busy running around after little Joseph. I had no idea how active a child his age could be."

The shadow that darkened Aidan's vision had nothing to do with the time of day. He shook it off and placed a hand on his friend's shoulder. "It really is good to see you."

"You, too, buddy." Dion lifted the six-pack out of the sack. "I thought we could relax and catch up."

Aidan groaned. "We can relax, but those" —he pointed at the beer— "are all for you."

Dion stared at him. "You don't look so good."

"I don't feel so good." Aidan headed for the kitchen. "I need some coffee."

A few sips of coffee and a couple aspirin helped Aidan's disposition—marginally. He'd found the bottle of whiskey. It was empty. The problem was, he couldn't remember how full it had been when he started. This was a first for him. No woman had ever driven him to drink before Gail.

Damn. He'd meant to call Hawk and Julia to check on Gail. She shouldn't be alone. Especially in her state.

"Back in a sec," Aidan said to Dion. In his bedroom he placed the call, but no one was home. He hated leaving a message but really had no choice. "Hey, Hawk, Julia. Umm, could you do me a favor? Gail should be home by now. Would you check on her and make sure she got in okay? I'd appreciate it. Well, I guess that's it. Catch you later."

After he hung up, he sat there for a long moment staring at the phone.

"So...you and that assistant of Julia's, huh?" Dion stood in the doorway.

"No. Well, at least, not anymore." Aidan brushed past his friend and grabbed his cup of coffee. "What's this charity event you've got going on?"

"Uh uh. You don't get off the hook that easily, pal. You two seemed pretty hot and heavy in Mexico. Now I hear you calling Hawk to check on her. And I can't remember the last time I saw you tie one on"—he lifted the empty bottle for effect—"this hard. Spill."

Aidan sat at the table and stared into his mug. He didn't want to get into it. Hell, he didn't even know where to start.

"She's pregnant."

Dion hooted as the sip of beer went spewing all over the table. He grabbed napkins and dabbed at the mess but still couldn't stop chuckling. "Welcome to the club, man." He clapped Aidan on the back, then stopped and took a good look. "You're not happy about this?"

"Very astute."

"Hey, I used to be in the spy business, remember? Astute is my middle name."

The levity fell flat as Aidan swirled his coffee. "Problem is, I'm not daddy material," he said quietly.

Dion tossed the soiled napkins in the waste bin and leaned against the counter. "Why not?"

"Just trust me. I'm not. And anyone I've ever dated has known that from the get-go."

"Really." Dion sat down at the table.

"Yes. Really."

"And you told Gail this."

"Yep."

"Then how did she get pregnant?"

The vision hit him square between the eyes. Gail, pink robe hanging off one shoulder, pinned against her front door by his need, his desire, his insatiable craving for her.

Dion read his delay in answering accurately. "So...it wasn't just her fault, then?"

"God, no. We'd been using protection. We just, uh, got caught up in the moment. One friggin' time. That's all it took, apparently."

"I know how that can be, my friend. Well, she's pregnant. The question is, what are you going to do about it?"

"There's nothing I can do."

"There's a lot you can do."

"Like what? She won't even consider options."

"I wouldn't expect her to. I do, however, think you owe her more than a brush-off."

"What the hell do you mean by that?"

"I mean, you got a girl pregnant and now you need to do the right thing and work this out *with* her. What the hell's wrong with you, man? This isn't you. This isn't the Aidan who did anything and everything he had to do to save my ass when I was down." Dion shoved his finger at Aidan.

Aidan could feel the rush of color flood his face. He clenched and unclenched his hands under the table to keep from decking his partner.

"You don't run and hide," Dion went on. "You scrape your way through. You don't talk much about your past, but I know enough to figure out that's where your problems lie. Gail is paying a price someone else set. And that's not very fair to her."

That was about all Aidan was going to take. He stood, turned to Dion with slow precision, and roared. "What the hell business is it of yours? If you can't keep your big mouth shut, then get the hell out of my place!"

"Yeah, yeah. I'm leaving. But I'm disappointed in you, buddy. I hope you get your head out of your ass and see the opportunity staring you in the face." Dion shook his head as he opened the front door. "You're better than this, man. Much better."

After Dion left, Aidan stood shaking with anger and no place to funnel it. He did the only thing he could. He ran. Long and hard, trying to lose the demons yapping at his heels. Even when exhaustion begged him to stop, he kept going. It didn't help. He still heard Dion's accusations. Saw the hurt in Gail's face. Hurt he put there.

Back at home, Aidan flopped on the bed. A baby. One he'd helped conceive. It couldn't be. Couldn't happen. He'd been so careful. Flashes of pink-infused passion made him pound his pillow in frustration. He hadn't been careful. He'd been reckless and full of a need he'd never felt before.

Even in this bed, that passion had fueled itself into combustion. He lost himself around her. His rigid control, so well hidden from everyone, shattered in her presence.

Aidan flew off the bed as if it burned him, grabbed his workout bag and lit out for the local gym.

Visions he thought he'd made peace with filled his mind. A mother's tears that had died with a needle full of heroin. A child who didn't understand, couldn't understand until so many years later, the reasons for her abandonment. Even then, the pain...

He'd vowed never to pass his family traits on. Never!

At the gym, he wrapped his hands, then unwrapped and re-did them when he realized they were too tight. If he didn't hit something soon he was going to explode. Aidan slammed on his gloves like they were his opponent and attacked the heavy bag with one jab after another. Each time the bag swung back he was ready with another punch.

Left jab. Right hook. One, two, one, two.

Why did she leave?

He threw his body behind each punch over and over again.

With every swing of the bag, he saw the little boy he'd once been, waiting in that mall. And he pounded the memory to a pulp.

Or tried to.

Left, left, left, then another right hook. Then back to the quick, quick, one, two, one two.

Panting, he hugged the bag while the vision of him as that boy being led away by child protective services flooded his mind.

Why? Why didn't I mean more to you than your next fix? Why wasn't I important enough for you to overcome your own past?

Pow! The bag went flying. As it returned for more abuse, he hit it with a couple more jabs.

Aidan thought about his mother and what he'd found out about the abuse her father had heaped on her. Abuse and abandonment were his legacy.

The bag rebounded and Aidan grabbed it, holding on as he worked to catch his breath. Was it his legacy? He saw his mother's face again as she left him. She'd been...sad. What had she said? That he'd be better off now? He smacked the bag. *Yeah, right.*

He collapsed on a nearby bench and wiped an arm across his sweat-soaked brow as he tried to work the thread of pain through to its conclusion. His mother had left him to go buy drugs and had died of an overdose that very night. She spent years escaping the memories. The beatings at the hand of her father. Had she given up? Or maybe she'd had some sort of premonition and wanted her final act to be that of protecting her son?

Aidan had chosen never to have children because he refused to subject them to what he'd gone through, what she'd gone through. He chose never to put himself in the position of becoming what his past destined he would. A monster.

Yet his mother had given him up before she turned into that monster. What if she'd chosen to give him up because she wanted him to have a chance at life without suffering through her legacy?

She'd protected him, the same thing he now did for his own unborn child, eliminating any chance that he would morph into something he abhorred.

She wasn't a monster. Her last act had been both selfish and selfless. He knew that now. She had chosen death to save him, to protect him. To give him the chance she'd never had.

Could he overcome his demons in a more positive way? Was he strong enough?

He'd already abandoned the one person who had found her way into his heart. He clutched his head in his gloved hands, digging for an answer that would stop this pain.

Aidan shot up, realizing the pain on Gail's face had mirrored his. Pain he'd caused by leaving her when things got tough.

He was the worst kind of heel. He'd abandoned Gail. He'd become his mother, and not by any damn hereditary trait. No, he'd done it consciously. Shit. He needed to talk to Gail. Needed to make this right. To tell her, show her he was the man she thought he could be.

Aidan yanked off his gloves, grabbed his gym bag, and headed for his apartment. The phone stopped ringing just as he let himself in.

Gail.

When it started ringing again, he lunged for it.

"We've got a situation."

It wasn't Gail. *Damn it.* It wasn't her.

"Director," Aidan said, collapsing down on the couch and trying to re-orient himself.

"I need you here. Now."

He ran his hand through his hair. "I can't. I need to—"

"You need to get your ass to IMB. Now."

Shit. Shit. Shit. Aidan scrubbed his hair with his free hand. Couldn't the world just stop spinning for one freaking day and give him time to sort this all out? Okay. He'd go to IMB. And he'd call Gail. Beg her to give him another chance. To not write him off until he could get to her.

"Yeah. Fine. I'll be there in half an hour."

"I've sent a car. It'll be there in ten minutes."

Aidan disconnected, then dialed Gail, but it went to voicemail. He closed his phone, knowing he couldn't say what he needed to say to a digital storage file.

He changed clothes and tried again. Again she didn't answer. He called Dion and left him a message. "You were right, man. Thanks. I owe you. And... I'll make it right. But I've been called out on an op. Get her to wait for me, okay?"

On the way to headquarters, he tried Gail's cell phone again, this time leaving a message. He had no choice. Time had stolen any options open to him.

"Gail. I'm sorry. I've been an ass. Listen, I... have to go somewhere, and I don't know when I'll be able to come to you. But I'll be there. We need to talk."

He hung up and stared at the phone, supremely unsatisfied. Why did his worlds always seem to collide? Couldn't they find a way to co-exist? He hit his head against the seat back. Shit.

CHAPTER THIRTEEN

Thirty-six hours and some serious begging later, along with her savings account pretty much drained, Gail arrived home. She let herself in, dropped her bags, switched her phone off, and slumped onto the couch. Pulling a comforter over her, she lay there in a tight ball, one hand on her stomach, the other wiping tears that refused to dry from her face. It took a while, but she finally drifted off into merciful slumber.

When she awoke, the fog didn't lift easily. Gail reached up to stop the hammer that was driving into her skull, one knock at a time. Except it didn't hurt. She touched different points on her head. No pain. When she opened her eyes, only the curtained light of day filtering in told her time had passed. Her suitcases stood unopened just inside the door where she'd left them.

She missed Pappy. And she wasn't relishing the explanation she'd have to give Julia in order to pick him up today. Still, it would be good to have him home. He seemed to be the only male who could love her unconditionally.

Sitting up, she heard the insistent pounding again. It was coming from the door. Gail stumbled out of the blanket, off the couch, and over to the offending portal.

"Who is it?" she grumbled.

"Gail, it's me. Julia. Let me in."

Gail groaned. How the hell did Julia even know she was home?

She flipped the lock and opened the door just as a wave of nausea hit her. She barely made it to the bathroom, an exuberant Pappy tight on her heels.

When she walked out a few minutes later, her living room had transformed itself from a tomb to something that resembled functional. The comforter sat serenely on the back of the couch, the drapes were open and San Diego sunlight streamed in. Plus, her suitcases...and her friend were nowhere to be found.

She found Julia in her bedroom, unpacking. Taking the makeup bag out of Julia's hand, Gail tossed it on the bed. "I don't need you to unpack for me."

Julia, wisely, didn't take her to task for the nasty tone. She patted Gail on the shoulder. "Come on. Tea should just about be ready. Let's take it out on deck."

Since Gail's apartment was on the second floor, her deck was more like a large step. There was just enough room for the little bistro set she'd found on clearance at the local hardware store. It baked in the afternoon, being on the west side of the apartment complex. But now, in the shade of mid-morning, it was comfortable.

"How are you feeling?" Julia asked.

"Fine."

Julia arched an eyebrow.

"No. Really. I'm fine. Probably just jet lag from all the recent flying I've done. Not something I'd recommend to, well, to anyone." Gail laughed, trying to steer her friend in a safer direction.

A few long moments of silence passed before the just-right warmth of San Diego worked its magic and Gail felt more like her old self. She turned to Julia. "How'd you know I was back?"

"Hmmm. A little birdie told me?"

"Meaning Aidan?"

Julia nodded. "Aidan's worried about you."

"He should be."

"I gathered that. So, you want to tell me what happened?"

Gail looked out over the courtyard before responding. "I'm pregnant."

"I know."

Gail stared at her. "How?"

Julia patted her own nicely rounded stomach. "I recognized the symptoms, although they seem to have hit you much earlier than my own did."

A hint of green tinted Gail's vision. Her best friend had it all. The looks, the high-powered job, the hunky husband and perfect marriage. And now, a family in the making. And a husband who wanted that child. Hawk was one of the most supportive, proud, overprotective men Gail had ever met. Gail had thought...no. No use rehashing that.

"At least you have someone to share it with."

"I take it Aidan didn't react well."

"That's putting it mildly. I've been told unequivocally not to expect any participation from him. 'My genes make me bad parent-material,' he said."

"Ouch." Julia patted Gail's hand. "Did he say why?"

She flashed to that little boy sitting all alone in the food court, waiting for a mother who would never return. "He didn't have the best past." Her tea mug clunked as it hit the glass table. It was a wonder neither broke on impact. "But a lousy past is a pretty rotten excuse for ignoring a present...and a future."

Julia looked as if she wanted to comment but held her tongue. Instead, she gripped Gail's hand. "You won't be going this alone. You've got me. And Hawk."

Gail pulled her hand out from underneath Julia's. "It's not the same."

"I know it isn't. And I'm going to hope and pray that Aidan comes through this with some new insights. Give him time. He's a good man, honey."

The sheen of new tears threatened as Gail prayed her friend would be right. "I thought so, too."

Julia stood and piled the tea dishes on a tray to take inside. "I think Aidan will come around. You wait and see." She waited while Gail opened the screen for her. "In the meantime," Julia continued, "there are things to do. Do you have an obstetrician? We should get you into one right away, especially as ill as you've been feeling. You look like you're losing weight. I'll call mine and set up an appointment for you."

Julia kept up the light chatter until she'd tidied up from tea. As she made to leave, she turned to Gail with worry evident in her face. "Do you want me to stay? I can."

Gail pulled her brave smile out of her magic hat and put it firmly in place. "Don't worry about me. I'll be just fine. Besides—" She held her head up. "I need to take Pappy for a walk. He's looking a little desperate and I've missed him."

"Ooh. Then I'm out of here. I never met a dog like him. He tolerated us but just barely. He doesn't seem to like anyone but you."

He learned to like Aidan.

With one last hesitation and a hug for good measure, Julia was out the door.

Gail closed it with relief, then looked around her empty apartment and wondered how she was going to do this whole baby thing in such a small place. It seemed even smaller now. Shabbier. Probably because Aidan had brought so much life to the place.

God, everything inside of her ached, and she doubted she could attribute that to the baby. Her heart felt ready to shatter. Maybe it already had. How could she fall for someone so quickly? How could she miss him this much?

She shouldn't miss him at all, but there it was. Her glum mood had a name. Aidan Walker. She gave herself one long moment to grieve for what could have been, then shoved it into the recesses of her heart. "I've got a life to live, Aidan Walker. And a new one to care for. If you're not interested in the love we have to offer, so be it. It's your loss."

Gail grabbed the leash. Pappy wore trails in the rug around her as she tried to get it attached. The effort almost made her give up on the whole thing. He could just pee on the rug. Her Schnauzer put his paws on her legs as she leaned over, gave her a sloppy lick on the cheek, then stood quietly so she could finally get him hooked and out the door. It was hard not to smile at his antics.

Still, Pappy's incessant enthusiasm couldn't completely dispel Gail's melancholy. Back home, she gave him a couple treats, then pulled out the proposal she'd taken to England to work on. She needed a distraction and this one, at least, gave her a chance at some forward momentum in her life.

Julia had promised her a shot at lead on the charity drive if her proposal was good enough. Gail hoped to get the coveted promotion to project manager if this went well. In fact, she was now banking on it. She placed a hand on her stomach with a little smile. She was going to need the money to take care of this baby.

CHAPTER FOURTEEN

Aidan walked into IMB headquarters with his cell phone glued to his ear. Four consecutive tries and still only voicemail. Damn it. *Pick up the damn phone, Gail.*

"About time, Walker." The director's voice boomed down the hall. "Where the hell have you been?"

"Busy," Aidan said, tight lipped.

"Well, get your priorities straight because you're about to be even busier."

Aidan gave his phone one last, lingering look and tucked it into his back pocket, following Director Chuck Ecker into his office. "What's up, boss?"

"We've got a missing yacht."

Aidan plopped onto the couch. "Okay. I don't mean to sound callous, but what's the big emergency about a missing yacht?"

"Because I can pretty much guarantee you this is a set-up designed to draw you out. And the yacht belongs to Senator Detson."

"*The* Senator Detson?" Aidan sat up. "The one who thinks we're pansy-asses when it comes to prosecuting pirates and wants to pull U.S. funding from the IMB?"

"That's the one."

"Okay. You've got my attention."

"It gets worse," the director continued. "It went missing near the Panama Canal."

"So why do you think there's a connection to me?"

The director turned his computer screen toward Aidan. "Because of this."

Aidan's blood turned to ice when he saw what the email said.

If you want to see your senator again: Dockside cantina, Puerto Amador. Tuesday. 4PM local. Send Walker. Alone.

"Shit," Aidan whispered.

"Yeah. The only good news is that we've ID'd the guy you pissed off. Carlos Salvena, drug lord to the max. That raid you took part in? The guy you killed? That was his son."

The words he'd heard uttered days ago screamed through Aidan's head and settled like a chunk of lead in his stomach.

I will find you. And I will spit on your grave.

Aidan tried to shrug off a chill as he remembered the man's parting words.

"So this is his play? This is how he wants to draw me out? I'm not sure I buy that this is all about him finding me."

Director Ecker nodded. "I agree, but it's all we've got to go on right now."

"Sounds like I'm heading for Panama."

"Absolutely not," the director boomed. "No way are we throwing you right in his path."

"You have to. You know what this guy'll do to the senator, and whoever is with him, if I don't show up."

"I do, but you're still not going there." The director reached to stroke a non-existent beard, then rubbed his chin instead. "Look, we need to move very cautiously here. I've got a handful of agents en route to the area. They'll act on your orders so I need you up to speed and using that intuition of yours."

"It's not my first choice, but okay. I'll review the intel and figure out a plan to proceed with."

"Do it quick, Walker. I don't have to tell you how many people are breathing down my neck right now, do I?"

"Somehow, I think you can handle it, boss." The lighter moment felt at odds with the situation, and Aidan's chuckle fell flat and left a bad taste in his mouth. He pulled his cell from his pocket and flipped it open.

"Who're you trying to get a hold of?"

Aidan hesitated while he decided how much to reveal to his director. "A woman."

The director frowned. "Someone important?"

"Maybe," he answered. This wasn't a discussion he wanted to have with the director. He wanted to be having it with Gail.

His boss's frown twitched as though he wanted to smile. "I was starting to think you weren't capable of having a real life."

"Yeah, well, don't start counting your chickens yet. I... may have screwed the pooch on this one." He winced as the truth hit him in the gut, sizzling like a hot iron.

The director motioned Aidan toward the door. "Just keep your focus in the right place. I don't need to remind you what's at stake here. This is a personal statement Salvena is making, so you'll need to be on your toes."

Dredging up a cocky grin, Aidan saluted the man. "Ah, it's so nice to know you care, boss."

Back in his own office, Aidan collapsed to the chair and stared at the cell phone in his hand. He set it down on his desk, his hand covering it for a long moment of regret. Where was she? And what was she doing at this moment? He'd hurt her, and that was killing him. Aidan scrubbed his chin, wishing like hell he could fix it now. Ease the pain Gail must feel.

The sooner this op was over, the sooner he could go to her. Aidan turned to his computer and pulled up the op files. Some researcher had named the op *Agent's Bane*. That's all the IMB would need, for that name to get out to the media. Aidan renamed it, and *Operation Return Salvo* was born.

He spent the next couple hours reading through the reports. The yacht had been working its way down the Pacific Coast, past Mexico. It stopped in San Jose, Guatemala, then wound its way toward the Panama Canal. When the senator's wife had tried to reach him for two days with no response, she'd contacted the authorities. When she told them he was there with another woman and she needed to serve him with divorce papers, they'd chosen to lay low, even though Detson was a senator. This disappearance had seemed tryst-related rather than an actual kidnapping.

At least, it had until this morning when that message had arrived. The shadow hovering over Aidan's desk for the past couple hours settled with a chilly thud on his shoulders. Oh, yeah. This was payback time.

Shit. Aidan leaned his elbows on the desk and rubbed his face, then looked again at the screen.

Send Walker.

Carlos Salvena definitely wanted revenge.

For the first time, Aidan's real name was out there. As an undercover operative, he could handle any situation without blinking. But now he didn't have some manufactured persona to hide behind. And that made him feel naked. Exposed.

And worried. But Aidan Walker, the man without a family, who'd never cared for anything other than the next adrenaline rush, now had a reason to worry.

He thought about Gail. He'd run from her. Now, he felt like he was on the edge of a precipice. His life would be different from this point forward no matter what decisions he made. And right now, he didn't have time to even think about those choices.

One thing was certain, though, Aidan thought as he picked up the phone to call the director. Despite how she might feel about him at the moment, Gail had feelings for him. And she would kill him if she found out just how far into harm's way he was about to argue that he needed to go.

Routine had provided the thin filament of thread that kept Gail from completely breaking down these last couple days.

Wake up.

Throw up.

Get dressed.

Throw up again.

Go to work and eat crackers until the waves of nausea subsided. All the while, her heart felt the world-ending loss of Aidan, offset by the awe-filled memory that there was a new life inside her. One that was part her, part Aidan. Her mind whirled at the incongruity.

Gail's office looked like a hurricane had whipped through it. There were binders in various stages of open and papers spread everywhere. She sat turned away from her desk, the cursor of her computer blinking behind her. Instead of working on the proposal that was due in a few short days, she stared out at the San Diego skyline.

It was as if Aidan had fallen off the face of the earth, job or no job. She'd never have believed he would just dump her like this. Granted, she didn't have the best track record at picking keepers, but he'd seemed so...real. Once again, he was just gone. A few attempts to call her, one quick "we need to talk" message, and then nothing. She'd tried to just let him go. Made it two entire days before returning his call, both to his apartment and his cell.

Not only had he not answered—he hadn't even bothered to find a way to call her back. One part of her wanted to shred the man. The bigger part—she placed a hand over her stomach—was glad some piece of him was still with her.

"How's that proposal coming?"

Gail twisted and glanced over her shoulder as her friend entered. Julia looked at the piles littering the two chairs and rounded the desk to lean against the windowsill.

"Need any help?" She waved a hand over the chaos.

"No." Gail sighed. "I'll get it done. And on time."

Julia patted her shoulder. "I know you will. I'm not worried. And..." She settled back onto the sill. "That's not why I'm here. I have some news."

The you're-not-going-to-like-this tone in Julia's voice got Gail's full attention.

"Hawk told me Dion called."

Gail leaned forward in her chair. "Aidan's old partner?"

"Yes. Apparently, he was in England."

Julia paused, which had Gail circling her arms in front of her to urge the woman to continue.

"He stopped by to see Aidan."

Again, Julia paused, causing Gail to prompt her one more time. "And?"

"And it sounds like your guy was in pretty rough shape."

Gail plopped back into her chair. "Please. The man didn't even bother to call me back after that first day."

"Not didn't. Couldn't. Dion found out he got called in. Another emergency op."

Gail's heart stopped for one infinitesimal moment. He'd put himself on the frontlines of danger again. Would he continue to dodge the bullets or would his luck run out?

Falling for a guy who ran in his dangerous circles was not good for her heart, her mind, or any other part of her. Gail worried her lower lip, wondering how deep he'd go with this op, and how long it would take.

No. He wasn't her problem anymore. He'd made that clear. Gail closed her eyes and visualized putting all her worry in a box. Then she screwed the box shut and filed it away in the recesses of her heart. Except the damn thing was overflowing and the worry still coursed through her veins.

She opened her eyes and gave Julia what she hoped was bravado. "I'm sure he's happy to be back in the thick of things. Seems to be his favorite place."

"Gail..."

"I don't want to hear it, Julia." Gail winced inwardly at the lie. But she needed to start her new life, not keep thinking about the past. "The man doesn't want anything to do with me. Plus, this isn't the first time he's put himself in danger and I'm betting it won't be the last. He appears to like danger a hell of a lot more than he likes me." Gail sighed. "I—I need to let him go or I'll drive myself nuts."

Julia looked long and hard at her friend before getting up to leave. "All right. I guess I can understand why you don't want to hear about him." She turned back to Gail at the door. "You know, it's just possible this op is what's kept him from being here with you. Give the man a little time. He'll come around."

Gail placed a hand on her stomach. "We don't intend to wait."

Julia looked like she had more to say but thought better of it, leaving Gail to her own thoughts.

Smart woman. Gail stabbed at her keyboard and forced her mind to focus on the proposal. It took a while, as the screws on the neatly tucked away box of worry kept trying to loosen. Something felt wrong. This was the second time in only a few short weeks he'd been called away on an urgent mission.

Damn it. She wasn't going to think about him anymore. She tried to focus, to read the screen in front of her. It took a while, but it eventually drew her attention. Since Thoralssen Industries, owned by Hawk and Julia Thoralssen, had gone philanthropic, she'd been part of many happy events. The corporation needed to make money in order to spend it, so there were two divisions to the company. The money-making side helped businesses about to go under to re-format themselves and become profitable endeavors again. The percentage of the profits they earned from that fed the humanitarian side, where Gail's very satisfying job was.

The proposal, her first, was a campaign to help teenagers and young women have access to birth control, along with pre and post intercourse counseling. In conjunction with a local organization, she proposed an idea that raised both money and awareness. It would start with an aggressive campaign showing that S.I.S., or Safety In Sex, did not counsel on pregnancy options. Instead, they tried to get the word, and the supplies, out to keep unplanned pregnancies from happening.

The irony of the situation didn't escape her. If she'd remembered those supplies... No. She wouldn't change a thing. This baby might not be planned, but she would welcome it. And work extra hard to make sure it was loved.

When it came to increasing awareness, like she needed for this campaign, it took money. So a series of expensive television ads were the first priority and a tough hump to straddle when charity dollars were at a premium. However, she argued in her proposal, after the initial outlay, Thoralssen Industries could ramp up a ground-floor movement through the internet and local radio stations that would cost next to nothing.

Gail had managed to get commitments from several well-known sources. She proposed that the company cover the cost of the initial television ads to "reset" the impression people had of S.I.S. After that, donations from other sources would take over and the organization could self-sustain with minimal oversight.

When Gail looked up again, the day had disappeared. Pinching her nose as she tried to re-focus from the computer to the world at large, she thought again about Aidan. Where was he and how much danger was he in?

CHAPTER FIFTEEN

After arguing with the director until he was hoarse, Aidan sat slumped at his desk. He should be in Panama. Hell, his partner, Mike, was even there. *He* should be on the front line for this op. It was killing him to sit here and wait.

Worse, something just didn't feel right to Aidan. He stared at his computer screen, then pulled up the satellite photos again. The first ones, from three days ago, showed the senator's yacht along the coast of Costa Rica, en route to the Panama Canal. His wife said he'd paid four times the normal amount for a preferential transit time. Yet the next pass of the satellite showed no sign of the yacht anywhere in the vicinity of the canal.

He grabbed a map. There were plenty of places a yacht could moor, but not without being seen. A yacht that size didn't just disappear. The wife, though, had been adamant her husband wouldn't spend that extra money and not transit. Colombia was on the east side of the canal. Glancing back at the earlier sat photos, they didn't show any other vessel around, or even near, the senator's yacht.

So where the hell was it? Frustration ate at Aidan. Mike and the team were ready to move at a moment's notice. Aidan should be there with them, but that damn "not only no, but hell no" record of the director's was stuck in repeat mode. Which meant Aidan was stuck behind a desk in England while his partner made ready to catch the bad guys. It sucked. Worse. In order to keep Salvena thinking they'd play along with his order, Aidan had been put in blackout mode. No contact with anyone, and that included Gail. He wanted to talk to her, to hear her voice, to tell her what an ass he'd been. God, he hoped she'd forgive him when this was all over.

No. He couldn't think about that now. He needed to solve this riddle first. Lives were at stake. So as hard as it was, he tamped down the worry and fear and tried, once again, to focus on the immediate problem. Aidan trailed his fingers along the western coast. Three days. That was more time than needed to get to the canal from Costa Rica. With no sign they'd moored to wait for transit, the yacht must have gone somewhere. A senator having a fling with another woman, the wife had said. Where would they go?

His finger stopped at Puerto Amador, where the meeting was scheduled. He tapped the map. It made sense that the senator and his lady friend might kill some time there. Aidan shot off a request for sat feeds from the area.

Bone-tired and unable to think, he lay on the couch in his office and shut his eyes. Sixty minutes later, he awoke alert and more certain than ever that his intuition was on the right track.

The sat feeds were in and Aidan whooped when he reviewed them. He'd been right. He ran to the director's office with the news, then the waiting began. Hours that Aidan could fill with nothing, since he was basically on lockdown. He paced. He tried to eat, but couldn't. He tried to focus on the backlog of reports that always perched precariously on his desk, to no avail.

Several hours passed before they knew the outcome. Long hours where Aidan almost broke dark mode on multiple occasions to call Gail. Hours where he had nothing else to do but berate himself for what he'd done to a woman he really cared about.

Finally, the call came in.

"We got them," Mike said over the sat phone. "They hadn't been kidnapped. They were just being watched while they played. We took out a couple of Salvena's men, boarded the yacht, and slipped away under darkness of night. The yacht's in open waters with a contingent aboard for safety. So the senator will be home soon to deal with the Mrs."

"Great job," the director said.

"Definitely," Aidan added. "Wish I'd been there with you, buddy."

Mike laughed. "Yeah, I know. Honestly, though, it was quiet as can be. Almost like Salvena didn't care all that much."

The hairs on the back of Aidan's neck ruffled. "It does seem that way."

"Could this have been a smokescreen for something else?" Ecker asked.

"I don't—" The chill wrapped around his neck and dove straight for his heart. Salvena knew his legal name. Could he know other details about his life?

"They could be after Gail." Aidan swallowed past the tight lump in his throat.

"Gail?" the director said.

"The woman— Ah, hell, I've got to go. I need to be in San Diego. Now."

The director nodded. "Go. And keep me in the loop."

Aidan hardly heard him. He was down the hall and gone in a flash, with only one thing on his mind.

Getting to the woman he loved.

CHAPTER SIXTEEN

No one answered the knock on her door. She wasn't home. He'd called Hawk and knew that Gail was all right. So why wasn't she here?

Aidan sat on the stairs, punching up her number on his cell. The call went straight to her voicemail. Damn it all. Where was she? He got up and paced, too keyed up to just sit and wait, wondering, praying she wouldn't refuse to talk to him. And knowing he wouldn't breathe easy until he saw her for himself, until he knew that she was okay. He didn't know where Salvena was, but all Aidan's instincts screamed that he wasn't very far away.

After the longest hour of his life, Gail walked around the corner, silhouetted by the sun's rays. Relief flooded him like that first spring rain, washing away the angst and worry. He marveled at how much he'd missed her. Even that short, spiky hair looked great. She was carrying bags, so she'd been shopping. When she saw the logo on the side, his smile faltered.

It said "Babies-R-Us."

She looked up then and caught him gaping at the bag. Gail stopped at the bottom of the stairs. He saw her eyes widen before returning to neutral and the mouth he'd so sorely missed become a thin line of anger.

He reached to take the bags.

Gail refused to release them. Instead, she trudged up the stairs and unlocked her door. Without giving him a chance to follow her, she turned in the doorway. "What do you want, Aidan?" Her voice dripped icicles.

He knew she'd be angry with him but had apparently underestimated the level of pissed she would be.

"We need to talk."

"I thought we pretty much said what we needed to say in England."

He glanced at the bag still in her hands, then back up at her face. "Can I at least come in?"

Gail stood there making him sweat for several long seconds before she finally backed away from the door, giving him entry.

Oh, yeah. She was about as pissed as a person could be.

She disappeared into her bedroom and left him standing in the living room. Rather than follow her—since that room held memories he'd need to keep tightly under wraps for now—he headed for the kitchen.

By the time she joined him, she'd changed into some gawd-awful pair of pajamas. What were those all over the pink material? Bunnies?

"I made you some tea." It sounded lame, even to him, but she settled into a kitchen chair, pulling her legs up underneath her. He poured himself a cup of coffee and sat across from her.

He took a sip and immediately regretted it as it scalded his mouth. After a quick trip to the sink and a few gulps of water, he sat back down, combing the singed texture from his tongue with his teeth.

All the while, Gail sat and watched without saying a word.

"We, um, didn't do too well the last time we talked."

"One of us didn't."

He caved. "You're right. I know I handled the whole thing badly."

"And then didn't call. Well, at least not beyond a couple hours of attempts and one lame message."

"There's a reason for that."

"For days."

"I know. I did try. A bunch of times."

"I didn't get any more messages." She took a sip of her tea and it about killed Aidan when he saw her hands shaking as she held the cup. He reached to help but pulled back, unsure how she'd take his offer.

"I... hate talking to voicemail. I tried. I left the one message. Then, I couldn't. Not until now."

"Yeah." Gail crossed her arms over her chest. "Let's see, what was that nice, long message you left? Oh yes, you said 'we need to talk.'"

"I didn't have time for much more. Geesh, Gail, you know my line of work."

He saw a crack in her armor as she nodded. "Yes. And Dion called Hawk, so I knew you were on an op."

"Then how in the hell did you expect me to call you?" Aidan scrubbed his hands through his hair in frustration How could they work this out if she shut him down every step of the way?

"I..." Gail picked up her teacup to take another sip. Her hands shook so badly, Aidan took it from her and set it down. He didn't let go of her hands, either. No more pussyfooting around their issues. She may not want to look at him, but they were going to address this head-on.

"Talk to me, doll. Please."

She stared at their hands. "I guess I wanted to be more important to you than some mission." She looked up at him then and the sheen in her eyes about undid him. "We left things so badly," she continued, "and then you up and disappear on some op with only one cryptic little message. Besides, it doesn't change the fact that you don't want my baby."

She pulled her hands from his and wrapped them across her stomach.

"I know what I said. I'd like to explain it, if you'll let me." Aidan took a guarded sip of his cooling coffee as Gail nodded.

"I would like to understand," she said, knowing she meant it. She really did want to know why Aidan couldn't get beyond the issues from his past.

"I don't talk about this. Ever," he said.

"I kind of figured that out."

"You know my mother abandoned me."

Her heart melted, just a little. "Yes."

"Look, I'm not saying I'm all screwed up because of it. It happens. And it happened to me. What I didn't tell you was that she died of a heroin overdose that same night. When I dug into it years later, I found out that after she left me there, she scored some drugs. Drugs that were the last straw her body could take. She died before I was even turned over to Child Protective Services."

Gail hugged her stomach. "That's a horrible thing for a boy of seven to go through."

He stopped for another sip of coffee and Gail took the moment to re-group. She pictured Aidan, the little boy. Alone.

Scared. Waiting for someone who would never return. "How long did you wait?"

"In the food court? Several hours. A nice lady" —he smiled and Gail could see the impact this woman's action had on him written on Aidan's face— "bought me some food and waited with me until the authorities arrived. It was fifteen years later before I found out the whole story. Her name was listed so I located her and got a chance to thank her for her kindness."

Gail placed her hands over his. "Ah, Aidan. That was a lovely thing to do."

"She said she never knew if she'd done the right thing, calling the authorities. I relieved her mind over the whole issue. It was worth the time it took to locate her."

"I can imagine." Gail realized her hands still covered his and she pulled them back to wrap around her cup. "It doesn't explain, though, why you reacted so strongly to the news that we" —Gail pointed to Aidan and then back to herself— "are going to have a child."

"I'm not finished." Aidan got up and started to pace the tiny kitchen. "You have to understand. My mom was a junkie. I have memories of at least five different dives we lived in, usually with whatever boyfriend she'd attached herself to for the moment. We moved all the time and never really had our own place. Mom got beat up. Often."

Gail gasped, but Aidan continued as if he hadn't heard.

"She seemed to like the dangerous ones. It took a lot of research to find out why."

Somehow, Gail knew. "She'd been abused by her father."

"Yes." The word came out in a long release of breath. "And that's why I've been so very careful not to father a child. Bad parenting is in my blood and I will not allow history to repeat itself."

"Aidan—"

"It happens every single day. This shit gets passed down the family line. I intended to break that line."

Gail nodded. "Except now, it's not so easy to say that, right? So you've had some time to get used to this change. I'm wondering what conclusions you came to." Gail waited, giving him time to digest the discussion, fear stopping the beat of her heart for long seconds as she waited.

Aidan leaned against the counter and ran both hands through his hair. Taking a long, ragged breath, he squatted down in front of Gail.

This was it. Gail knew that the next words out of his mouth would determine if they had a shot at a relationship and if her baby would have a full-time father. She realized she was holding her breath and let it out in a slow, controlled release as she waited.

He tapped his fingers on her knees as he looked at her. "I truly believe I am not good parent-material."

She scrunched her nose, wanting to refute his statement, but he held up a hand to forestall her.

"Only time is going to change that belief." A quick smile hit his face as he ran a hand along her cheek. "There's one other thing I know. I want you in my life, Gail. In fact, these past few days, imagining the opposite, have been pretty bleak."

Hope trickled into Gail's heart like the warmth of an early spring sunrise.

"So—" Aidan continued. "I'm hoping you'll give it a try. I mean, us. I'd like to be part of your life. And the baby's. If you'll still have me."

She should stay ticked off. She had every right to, but holding on to anger wasn't Gail's style, especially with someone as important to her as Aidan was. Any remaining anger trickled out of Gail's body as Aidan said the words she had cried herself to sleep wishing she would hear. As relief bubbled up inside her, she erupted off the chair and into Aidan's arms.

He clutched her to him, burying his head in her neck. "I'm so sorry, doll."

"It's all right, Aidan." Gail pulled back and clasped his face in her hands. "I could have been more understanding, too. Everything's all right now. God, I've missed you." She wrapped her arms around him again and laughed.

"And I missed you. Your smile. And your laugh and sharp wit. And everything else, including this exceptional body of yours." He nuzzled her neck. "So..."

She could feel his smile against her skin and a shiver of need coursed through her.

"Want to kiss and make up?"

"More than just about anything," she answered. When he started to move them to the bedroom, she stopped him. "First, I need some dinner."

Aidan groaned, even as his stomach gave him away with a loud growl.

Gail laughed. "See? You need food, too."

Aidan looked down at his stomach. "Traitor."

"Come on. Let's go get some dinner. After all, I'm eating for two."

Gail froze in place as Aidan's smile faded. "I'm sorry," she said. "I guess it's a little too soon to makes jokes about it."

Aidan then did something so totally unexpected, it brought tears to Gail's eyes. He got down on one knee and placed a hand gently on her stomach.

"Hey, little guy. I'd like to introduce myself. I'm your dad. I don't know if I'll be any good at this, but you deserve a mother *and* a father. You're a part of me. And I want you to know that I'll give it my best shot." He stole a quick glance at Gail.

"Besides, someone has to show you that women do *not* rule the world."

"Like that's going to happen. Besides, who says it's going to be a boy?" Gail swatted him with one hand as she wiped tears with the other.

Standing, he laughed. "Then I'll be sure she knows that the fairer sex really does rule." He held up his hands. "I know, I know. Double standard, right?"

It was Gail's turn to laugh as he asked her where she wanted to eat. They were out the door in minutes. While Aidan stood scanning the street, she glanced back into her apartment before closing the door. Somehow, it looked larger, happier, and no longer like a dungeon. She smiled and linked her arm through Aidan's, knowing the world would be fine now.

CHAPTER SEVENTEEN

Gail woke up the next morning to a warm body snuggled up to her. For the first time in weeks, she didn't have to rush to the toilet. *You like having him here, don't you, baby?* She smiled as she rubbed her belly.

Then she glanced at the clock. Damn. She had a 9:00 a.m. meeting and she was going to be late.

A hand covered her breast and fingers pinched her nipple, sending tingling waves of desire all over her body. Steeling herself against what had become an overwhelming need to stay in bed with her lover, she slapped Aidan's hand.

"I'm late for work. I've got to go."

He pulled her tighter against him and added soft kisses along her neck and upper back to his persuasion technique.

The tingle had now settled low in her spine and was sending radiating signals lower. She arched her back and stretched, bringing her breast close enough for Aidan to claim her with his mouth.

A gasp turned into a moan as he kissed her, his hand now free to roam. And roam it did, first to her other breast, then her ribcage, then lower. And lower. With soft, slow, tortuous strokes.

A feathered touch was all it took to work her into a frenzy. The man could damn near make her come with just a look. When he finally slipped his fingers inside her, all thought of work fled as she tipped over the edge and spiraled into oblivion. It was several long moments before she could breathe normally again.

"Now," Aidan said quietly in her ear, "what was that about work?"

As she turned to face him, Aidan marveled at the look of complete satisfaction on her face, fully aware that the half-mast eyes, slight smile, and still heaving bosom were there because of his actions. For the first time that he could recall, giving a woman pleasure was gratifying enough without ever going further.

He smiled as her hands encircled him. Of course, it was always nice when it went both ways.

Later, Gail whispered in his ear. "Now look what you've done. There's no way I am going to make my meeting now."

"Good. Then you can spend the day with me."

She pretended to think that over as she ran her fingers through the light tuft of hair on his chest. "Hmmm. Well, that certainly has some benefits to it. But you're not off the hook, mister. I've at least got to stop by and pick up some work. I'm on a deadline with a proposal and, thanks to you, will have to work evenings to get it done in time."

Gail tapped him lightly on the cheek. "Now go be the sweet guy you are and make me some tea while I check in with my boss."

The relegation to beverage server didn't bother Aidan a bit as he pulled on his jeans and went to do her bidding. Gail joined him moments later, still on the phone and wrapped in her pink satin robe. How many nights had he lain in a waking dream as he untied that sash and pulled the robe apart to reveal her to him?

He noticed then that the pink wasn't limited to the robe. It had crept up her neck and into her cheeks. He wondered what kind of grilling she was getting from her boss.

He frowned. If she was in trouble, he'd have to find a way to make it right. He'd met Julia in Mexico and had thought she and Gail were friends. Aidan wasn't beyond using that to make certain Gail didn't lose her job.

She hung up the phone and busied herself setting cream and sugar out.

He tipped her head up. "Are you in trouble at work?"

She gave a quick laugh. "No. Not at all. Julia was, um, fine with my taking the day off."

He stroked her cheek. "Then why the high color?"

The question alone heightened her blush to a furious level. "No reason."

"Come on, doll. What's got you going all shy on me?"

She batted his hand away. "It's nothing. She just...guessed my reason for calling in so late."

Aidan threw his head back and hooted.

"I don't think that's one bit funny. My love life is my own privileged business and I don't appreciate it being outside knowledge."

"You're wrong, you know."

She frowned. "About what?"

He fingered the edges of her robe, something that was fast becoming his favorite thing to do. Pulling apart the edges a bit, he peeked inside. "You're wrong that it's yours alone. It's ours now. We share in the pleasure."

Her blush was enhanced by a glow as her eyes melted under his gaze. "Oh, yes," she said. "We definitely share the pleasure."

He pulled the robe a bit farther apart and she slapped his hands. "But not right now. Breakfast, showers, and errands come first. I at least have to pop into work for a while."

"We have to do *all* of that before we can play?"

"Yep." She stirred her tea and took a satisfying sip. "Ummm, this is good." She frowned. "This isn't my usual tea?"

"Nope. I brought it from my place. You seemed to like it."

"Umm, hmmm. I like it a lot. Now go shower while I whip up a nice vegetarian scramble. It's my specialty." She ducked her head and mumbled, "My *only* specialty."

"Oh, Lord," Aidan said as he left the kitchen. "I can see I'm going to be doing the lion's share of the cooking." He poked his head back around the corner with a devilish grin. "Any interest in scrubbing my back?"

"A *lot* of interest. But it isn't going to happen. Now shoo!" She waved her hand, dismissing him.

Aidan headed for the shower, his deep, joyful laugh echoing behind him.

Gail dug in the fridge for eggs and other ingredients, surrounded by the warm feeling that Aidan's laughter left behind.

Later, showered and ready to go, Gail decided to test the water. "Are you ready?"

"Sure," he said as he held the door for her. "Let's go."

"No. I mean are you ready to officially present ourselves as a couple?"

She held her breath as he stood and stared at her without answering. Her breath whooshed out as a rakish smile spread across his face. "Since I doubt very much that I can tie you to the bed and never leave the apartment, I think I'm stuck with being seen out in public with you."

Gail rewarded him with a sweltering kiss, after which he licked his lips.

"Although, I am stronger than you. Maybe the whole tie-you-to-the-bed thing could work." He tried to turn back into the apartment but, with a laugh, Gail nudged him out the door.

They arrived at the headquarters of Thoralssen Industries and Gail buzzed them in with her card. Before they'd had a chance to settle into her office with coffee, Julia caught up to them, her husband firmly in tow.

Gail groaned and rolled her eyes as her boss entered. "Hi, Julia, Hawk. To what do I owe the pleasure of this visit?" She stayed purposely focused on Julia, and her friend had the good grace to at least look a little sheepish.

Hawk, never one to let an opportunity to tease his wife pass by, answered. "My wife, here, has been chomping at the bit to meet you, Aidan. Good to see you again."

Aidan shook his hand, grinning. "Better than last time. I am glad you didn't turn out to be the unsavory pirate we thought we were chasing."

"That's right," Gail said to Hawk. "Aidan arrested you at one point, didn't he?"

"Yes," Hawk said, shaking Aidan's hand. "But I promise I won't hold that against him."

"You led us on a pretty good chase, though," Aidan said, laughing.

"Oh, I know," Julia chimed in. "You two should come over for dinner. It would be a chance to reminisce and catch up on old times."

Gail started to protest, then decided what the heck. It would be fun. "What do you think, Aidan? Up for a little mixed company?"

The look he shot her had her feeling weak all over. Maybe dinner wasn't a good idea. Maybe they should just go home. Right now. Aidan's earlier statement about wanting to tie her to the bed was a great visual. Gail sank down in her chair, afraid her legs would give out.

"We'd love to," Aidan answered on their behalf. "What time and what can we bring?"

After they left, Aidan turned to Gail, who stared at him open-mouthed. "Guess we've jumped into the couples' pool with both feet, eh?"

"Yes," Gail answered. The problem was, now she wanted nothing more than to go home.

Aidan's phone rang. He glanced at it and frowned, then looked at Gail. "Why don't you get your work finished. I'll step outside to get this and be back in a few minutes, okay?"

"'kay," she answered, her gut churning. She watched him leave the office, wondering if this was how it would always be. Would she always be waiting for that next phone call?

True to his word, Aidan was back in only a few minutes, although he seemed distracted. He sat quietly and used his phone to check emails while she pulled together what she needed to work from home. The problem was, Gail was having just a bit of trouble focusing.

Gail placed both hands face down on top of the papers on her desk. It was as if her libido was at war with her heart. And her heart was currently filled with unease. Did the call mean he would leave again? A part of her wondered just how much of this come and go she could take, no matter how much she loved the man.

The jerk of her hands sent papers flying everywhere. Aidan smiled at her as he helped her pick them up, then resumed his work. She blushed crimson.

Did she love Aidan? She couldn't. She hadn't uttered those words in, well, several years. That last time, she'd thought it was love. Turned out, she was the only one who had believed in forever love. She knew, if she ever fell for someone again, she'd take her time, get to know them before falling off the edge. If you put all the actual time spent together back-to-back, she'd only known Aidan a few days.

She watched him tap away on his small keyboard. She certainly had trouble keeping her hands off him. But that was physical. Scratching a need, right? Yet, when he wasn't around, she had difficulty concentrating, her thoughts constantly drifting to him, to when she'd see him next. She glanced down at the mess of papers on her desk. Hell, she had trouble with concentration when he was right in front of her.

Maybe this was love. Maybe not. Only time would tell. For now, though, she was getting next to nothing done. It was time to get out of here. She stuffed the papers into her briefcase and pulled the jump drive out of the USB port on her computer.

"I'm ready anytime you are," she said to Aidan as she stood.

"Good." He joined her and took the briefcase out of her hand, checking his watch. "We've got some time before dinner, so how about we stop at the store and stock up on groceries? Your cupboards are still remarkably bare."

"I did explain, I believe up front, that cooking is not my strong suit." She was proud of herself for keeping her voice even. She was still reeling from the revelation she'd just had.

The home of Hawk and Julia Thoralssen downplayed their wealth. It was in a gated community, but Aidan would describe it more as comfortable than upscale. A stucco two-story in muted colors, the lawn was manicured with landscaping that didn't stand out.

A relaxed Hawk, in the shorts and tank top Aidan was used to seeing, greeted them. With a quick peck on Aidan's cheek, Gail left them and wandered off to help Julia in the kitchen. Aidan followed Hawk past comfortable southwestern style colors and overstuffed chairs to a deck that looked out across a spacious yard privatized by trees that had grown hedge-like over the years. The well-maintained lawn gave way to a few patches of garden.

Aidan clapped Hawk on the back as the man handed him a whiskey. "You're looking mighty urbanized, my man."

Hawk motioned him to one of the cushioned deck chairs. "It's not Tierra Bonita. Our hearts will always call the village home. This works well for when we have to be city dwellers. And the way Julia is working on the nursery, I may never get her out of the house again."

Aidan sobered. "Gail's pregnant."

"I know. Julia let it slip. Seems she recognized the symptoms before Gail did." Hawk reached over to shake Aidan's hand. "Congratulations."

"Yeah. Thanks." Aidan stared out at the yard but couldn't quite hide his concern.

"You're not happy about it?"

"It's sudden. I've got to get used to it."

"Why do I sense there's more to it than that?" Hawk asked.

"There is. It caused a big blow-up between us and we've only just gotten past it."

"So what's the problem?"

"I just...I've never considered myself to be quality parent material."

"Hell, is that all? We all go through that. Trust me." Hawk held up his beefy hands. "Don't you think I'm worried about crushing our son with these?"

Aidan chuckled. "I'm sure you'll do just fine."

"Fine with what?" Julia posed the question as she carried out a tray of food.

Hawk jumped up to take the tray from her and Aidan nabbed the one Gail was carrying. The table was quickly set and, before long, they were all passing around Caribbean jerk chicken, rice, and fruit salad under the spacious umbrella. Aidan served up the garden burger reserved for Gail.

"How did I ever hook up with someone who doesn't like meat?" He shook his head.

"I never said I didn't like it," Gail said. "I said I made a lifestyle choice and don't eat it."

"Oh ho! That means you can be tempted."

She smiled at him. "You relish meat enough for the both of us."

"True, true." He speared a second piece of chicken. "I do enjoy a good—"

"Side of beef!" Gail hooted as she finished his sentence. "I don't know how you stay so slim."

His eyes gleamed as they held hers for a long moment. "Lots of exercise, doll. Lots of it."

The rosy glow that transformed her face delighted him. She started to push her food around the plate, so he decided to cut her some slack and turned to Hawk. "How goes the corporate world?"

"It's amazingly complicated. I still feel like I'm at the beginning of a massive learning curve."

"Don't let my husband fool you. He's got a natural head for business." Julia poked Hawk in the ribs. "After his father's ruthless regime and subsequent demise, Hawk had a lot of cleaning up to do. Thoralssen Industries is thriving, thanks to him. And doing a lot more good than it used to."

Hawk placed a hand over his wife's. "As long as she keeps me out of jail, I manage to do okay."

Aidan remembered his role in Hawk's arrest. The man had taken to stealing yachts to finance the rebuilding of a village decimated by a mudslide. "I'm glad you've found legal ways to do your good deeds. It's a hell of a lot less paperwork for me."

Everyone laughed, then they all carried dishes into the house. Hawk and Aidan returned outside. Aidan's mind couldn't quite release the problem he'd been trying to work through all afternoon. The phone call from Director Ecker had unsettled him.

"You're worried about something other than Gail and the baby, aren't you?"

"Yes."

"Care to talk about it?"

He paused. Technically, it wasn't classified information. But discussing ops outside the bureau was not exactly something one did if they wanted to further their career. Still, an outsider's thoughts might help. "I've been working a case that involves a drug czar."

"From Colombia?"

"Yes. We managed to put a major crimp in his operations a few weeks ago."

"That's good."

"Definitely. Then, this last trip, we got wind of this possible kidnapping of a well-known politician. We almost took the bait but...well, something didn't sit right. Finally figured out the person had taken a detour. He hadn't been kidnapped. Our bad guy only capitalized on the handy delay.

"It's not easy, what you do."

"No. But this one seemed..." Aidan shook his head. "It *was* planned to involve me personally. And with this news today, I just don't know what to think." Aidan swirled the whiskey in his glass. What the hell did Salvena have planned?

"What news?"

"Sources indicate the man we've been struggling to apprehend entered the United States."

"What's so abnormal about that?"

"The fact that he has *never* been seen outside of Colombia."

"Oh," Hawk said. "And you're worried that he's here on some sort of vendetta?"

There it was. The real reason he felt an urgent need to find the Colombian. "Yes," he answered.

Hawk lowered his voice. "Do you think Gail is in any danger?"

Aidan clamped the lid tightly on the vision that tried to form in his head. "No. At least, I can't find any reason she should be. I live in England. We've only been together a short time and no one I know, with the exception of you and Dion, knows where she lives. Or," he said and then paused, "how serious we've become."

"But you're still worried."

"Yes. I can't help but feel I'm missing something." He paused again. "There's one more thing."

Aidan took a stiff swig of his drink as Hawk waited.

"He came in through Mexico."

"That sounds like a natural direction to come in from?"

"The only reason we know where he came across is because a photo was captured of him." He took another drink. "That in itself is unusual. The man is a recluse. Only someone in a hurry—or on a mission—would make that kind of mistake."

"Yeah. I remember trying to cross the border illegally. It's not easy."

"Right. It reeks of desperation."

Hawk frowned. "Where did he come across?"

Aidan took a deep breath. "California."

"Here?" Hawk stood up. "He's here?"

"We don't know. They lost him shortly after he entered the States. But yes, they believe he's somewhere in Southern California."

"Does he know your identity?"

"Yep. And he got a good look at me when I almost captured him."

"I'm guessing he's got a lot of connections. He'll find you, won't he?"

"More than likely he already has. Hence the worried look." Aidan pointed at his face.

Whatever discussion Gail and Julia were having had escalated and their laughter wafted out through the open window to the men. Aidan stepped off the deck and walked through the yard, with Hawk close by.

"I've decided not to tell Gail."

"I don't think keeping her in the dark is a great idea, Aidan."

"She worries too much."

Hawk glanced back at the house. "I know something about having someone special worry about you. Trust me, it's nice."

Aidan waved a hand. "I can take care of myself."

Hawk shook his head but kept his thoughts to himself. "What can I do to help?"

"She'll kill me herself if I hover too much." He smiled. "Not that she minds me being by her side. But I'll slip into bodyguard mode too often and she'll know something's up. She's got this uncanny knack for seeing right through me." Aidan shook his head.

"I definitely know what that's like," Hawk said with a grin. "Not necessarily a bad thing, but...disconcerting at first."

"You've got that right. Anyhow, can you keep an eye on her at the office?"

"Not a problem. Folks are screened pretty well coming in, but I can easily find a reason to post an additional security guard on our floor."

"I noticed the guys in your lobby don't look like your run-of-the-mill security guards."

"They're not. After my father passed away, we had some issues with some disgruntled former owners of companies he'd taken down. I beefed up security at that point and never really backed it off."

"That's going to help a lot. I don't have a car here, so don't have to contrive a reason to drive her to work."

Hawk rested a hand on Aidan's shoulder. "I still think you should tell her. She's got a lot of strength that you're not giving her credit for."

Aidan shook his head just as Gail and Julia walked out on deck with another tray of food, this time dessert. The next hour was spent in pleasant discussion of everything from work to world problems.

Before they left, Julia pulled them upstairs for a look at the nursery. Awash in all things boy, Aidan and Gail laughed as Julia pointed out item after item after item.

"She's not excited at all, is she?" Aidan asked Hawk.

"Not so much, no." Hawk grinned and pulled his wife into his arms. "It's time to let our guests return to their own lives, wife."

Julia blushed. "I'm sorry. I get a little overzealous."

"Not at all," Gail answered. "I'm taking notes."

CHAPTER EIGHTEEN

After saying their goodbyes, Gail realized just how tired she felt and handed Aidan the keys to her car. He kept a close eye on the mirrors on the way home, which seemed strange. She chalked it up to being in an unfamiliar area as she gave him directions for the final couple turns to her apartment.

They traversed the parking lot, with Aidan acting like one of those bobble-headed dogs, his head bouncing all over the place.

"What is up with you?"

"What do you mean?" He watched a car pass by on the side street.

"I mean, you've gone all security guard on me. What's up?"

"Nothing."

She waited until they were inside, set her purse down, then turned on him. "It's not nothing, Aidan. All of a sudden, you're uber-vigilant. And you've been on edge ever since you got that phone call today."

"Seriously, it's nothing," he said, heating up coffee in the microwave. "Do you want some tea?"

"No. I want some answers."

Aidan remained silent.

"You're leaving again, aren't you." She didn't bother making it a question. She already knew the answer.

"No. At least, not right away."

"When?"

"I don't know. Right now, what I need to do, I can do from here."

"Why do I feel that what you 'can do here' has something to do with me?"

Aidan pulled his coffee out of the microwave and took a sip. It was too hot and he sloshed it onto the counter, taking several hissing breaths as he waited for the sting to die away.

Gail watched and waited in silence. The man was holding out on her and she wanted information.

He looked up from cleaning the slopped coffee off the counter. "What?"

"I'm waiting for you to tell me what's going on."

"How many times do I have to say it? There's nothing going on."

Gail stared at him for several moments, then went into the bedroom and shut the door behind her. She tossed her wrap on the bed and plopped down on the chaise, almost missing it. She didn't remember moving it closer to the window.

How in the hell were she and Aidan supposed to have a relationship when he couldn't even answer a simple question?

She leaned her head against the back of the lounger and stared outside as the real question took root in her mind. Was he distracted and over-protective because of some perceived danger?

She didn't hear the door open so much as feel Aidan's presence. She refused to look his way as he sat down on the edge of the chaise lounge and took her hand.

"I'm sorry, doll."

"Are you going to tell me what's going on?"

"There are things I'm not at liberty to tell you. Isn't it enough that I'm not planning to leave anytime soon?"

She pulled her hand out from his and glared at him. "Those two things, the secrets and the sticking around thing? They don't usually go together. And I learned that *first* hand from a father with roaming hands and from a husband who had eyes for just about everyone but me."

Crap. She'd spilled it all out now. Gail turned back to the window, sticking her chin out.

She had to give him credit. He didn't flinch. His lips kind of disappeared into thin lines and his skin tone darkened, but he didn't move a muscle. "You mentioned before that you were married."

She didn't look down, didn't stare at her hands. She looked him in the eye. "Yes."

"I never got the full story."

"You got most of it, but we haven't had a lot of time to just sit and talk, Aidan. Either you're gone or we're in bed doing things that make discussion impossible."

A smile touched his face. "Yeah. So, when?"

"The divorce was final over a year ago, but the marriage, if that's what you want to call it, had been over long before that."

"What happened?"

"In a nutshell? He screwed around on me during our honeymoon, and that was only the first of many."

Aidan's skin darkened further with a flush, and a tiny tick started up near his eye. With a low voice that said how close to the edge he was, he asked his next question. "Why the hell did he marry you, then?"

"Beats me. You'd have to ask him. The point I'm trying to make here, Aidan, is that I don't do well with secrets."

"That is not fair. This is a totally different situation." He held her gaze. "And I am not your ex."

"Secrets are secrets in my book."

"Okay," he said slowly. "I, however, have not given you any reason to doubt me. I've been honest with you."

Brutally, in some respects.

"Trust is earned."

Mr. Cocky Attitude appeared, apparently trying to deflect the situation. "It's all good, doll. Really. I don't want you to worry," Aidan said.

"I'm going to worry no matter what. I love you." *Crap. Did I say that out loud?*

He squirmed in place, as if there were a burr under his thigh.

Oh, yeah. She'd said it out loud. Apparently, her brain had decided it was time to get *everything* out into the open, much to her heart's chagrin.

He didn't cower or look away, thank goodness. In fact, cocky flew out the window as concern replaced it. After a few interminable seconds, he reached out and began to rub her arms.

"I heard what you said. I'm not ignoring it, just so you know. Just...processing."

"I... didn't plan on saying that. At least, not yet."

"I know." He continued to move his hands up and down her arms. "I don't want there to be any more misunderstandings, so I'm going to be honest here."

Oh, God. Here it comes. He didn't return her feelings. Gail felt the pain swell in her like an allergic reaction run amok. Her skin felt tight, as if at any moment she might burst. Her heart felt the same way. Then the tremors started. He didn't return her feelings. She struggled to keep her arms still, while inside she felt as if she were exploding apart.

"You're shaking," Aidan said. He pulled her forward into his arms. With his face in her neck, he whispered words that began to soothe her soul. A little.

"Don't worry. I'm not going to run like a chicken from the hatchet man."

She chuckled, but still held on to him for dear life.

"I don't take what you said lightly. Love is a word I've not had much use for in my life."

Well, that's not too bad so far. At least he wasn't running for the hills. Her body stopped trembling and she loosened her hold on him.

"I care for you. More than I've ever cared for anyone."

Even better. Gail relaxed against his shoulder.

"I'm asking for some time. Time to sort this all out in my head. And in my heart. Time to...feel more comfortable letting you see a side of me I've kept boxed up for most of my life. Can you understand that?"

She nodded her head. "Yes."

"And you'll give us some time?"

She pulled back and touched his cheek. "All the time you need. The truth you've just told me...well, no one has ever given me a gift like that. This kind of honesty, I can definitely live with." She kissed him. "Thank you."

She kissed him again, this time slower and longer. Midway through, she stopped short and pulled back.

"Wait a minute. I'm still mad at you."

Aidan's face inched from budding desire to scrunched-up confusion. "What for?"

"Because you won't tell me what's going on."

"Damn," he said. "Doesn't the whole opening-myself-up count for anything?"

"Maybe. A little. Okay, a lot. But Aidan? Your job is going to be an issue for us if you have to continue this whole 'need to know' thing."

Aidan stiffened and Gail placed a hand on his arm. "I'm not trying to make you feel guilty about your job."

He stared at her with I-don't-believe-you written all over his face.

"Okay, so maybe I am a little. Look, I'm not an idiot. Something has you spooked. I think I have a right to know what it is."

He didn't respond right away but rubbed his hand over hers, back and forth. She waited impatiently.

"I don't want to worry you," he said again.

"We've been over this. I'm going to worry no matter what."

He took a deep breath. "Someone I've had dealings with, someone bad, has crossed the border into California."

"Okay." Gail drew the word out like it was a lifeline. "So maybe I will worry a bit more."

"See?" He tried for a smile, but to Gail it looked more like a lop-sided contortion. "I told you so."

"Who is after you?"

"I didn't say he was after me."

"Pul-lease," Gail said, rolling her eyes. "I *can* read between the lines, you know."

"I had a hand in thwarting a major move of his, so yes, he might be searching for me." Tight lipped, he stood and went into the bathroom.

Gail knew instinctively that she wouldn't get any more from him. She all but shook with frustration because she wanted to yank the information out of him. This weird code of silence that surrounded his job was going to drive her nuts.

Her brows rose as she considered the other side of the coin. If he was worried about her worrying about him, he wouldn't be as focused as he needed to be. Some instinct in her knew that he would need to concentrate hard to get them through whatever kind of mess this situation was.

And she needed to help him with that, which meant shutting her mouth and letting him play the man-guard.

Something that would be very, very hard for her to do.

When Aidan returned to the bedroom, he found Gail sitting on the side of the bed. She opened her arms to him and he walked into them. It felt more like home than anything he'd ever experienced. As Gail settled her head against his stomach, an new feeling warmed him. Awe. Maybe, just maybe, she was the one.

He leaned down to cup her face, turning her lips up to meet his. Deepening the kiss, warmth gave way to a slow building fire that carried them through the night.

In the morning, Aidan awoke to empty space beside him.

Gail!

Panic ejected him from the bed like a geyser, the gun he'd snaked under his pillow during the night now in his hand. His heart thudded in his chest as his gaze scanned the room. The bedroom looked untouched. He sidled over to the bathroom. Also empty.

Crash!

Aidan whirled toward the door just in time to see the last of the tray of eggs, bacon and coffee bounce as gravity yanked it to the floor, breaking dishes along the way.

"Shit," Gail screamed through the hand covering her mouth. "Where the hell did that gun come from?"

Aidan relaxed his stance and lowered his weapon, but not soon enough. Gail's widened eyes proved how much he'd shocked her. He set the gun on the bedside table and side-stepped the food to get to Gail, who stood like a zombie, unmoving, still staring at the spot he'd vacated.

"I'm so sorry, doll. I woke up and you weren't there. I thought..." What the hell could he say? I thought you were gone? I thought they'd taken you?

Her pale face deepened with anger as she threw off his arms. "You thought what? That I was in some sort of danger?" Pappy had started to dig in on the food. "Pappy! There's broken glass in there. Get away!" Gail shoved him in the spare bedroom and slammed the door. Dropping to her knees in front of the mess, she started tossing food onto the tray. "So you brought a *gun* into my apartment without telling me?"

She stood and marched out, returning shortly with a wet rag. She dabbed at the coffee-stained rug furiously as she worked herself into a state. Aidan tried to take the rag from her, but she whipped it away and continued to stab at the floor.

Aidan got another rag, plus some carpet cleaner he'd seen under her kitchen sink, then went back and nudged her out of the way. "You're going to wear a hole in the carpet," he said.

Gail slumped against the wall while he worked at what little remained of the stain. Then he sprayed the carpet cleaner on what was left. After a couple of good rinses with a fresh rag, the floor looked slightly wet, but unstained.

Only then did he look at her. Her face had lost its color, the anger replaced by another, more worrisome, emotion. Gail's eyes were wide and unstaring, as if she were grappling with some hidden demon.

He knew the look. Had, in fact, seen it on many occasions.

Fear. Aidan pulled her into his arms. "I'm sorry. I never meant for you to see the gun." She clung to him for several long moments. Her voice, when she spoke, was surprisingly strong. A good sign, in his mind.

"Just how afraid should I be, Aidan?"

He gave in. She had a right to know. So he told her. About the original op, and the trap that he'd almost walked into. He told her where illegals normally crossed the border, but this guy had crossed as near to here as possible, it seemed.

He could feel her reaction. Feel her arms tightening around him like a vise. Feel her shuddering breath when he glossed over the fact that he'd almost been duped by a drug lord.

When he was finished, the silence felt like that absolute kind of quiet just before a storm rages through. Both their chests rose and fell in sync, but he couldn't hear the sound of their breathing. He did not want to see the fear in her eyes. She would need time to come to terms with these events and get her fear under control. He understood that, so it surprised him when Gail pushed off him and stood, eyes glittering with fierce unshed tears.

"So, how do we find this badass and put him away for good?"

Shock hit him like a gale-force wind and kept him rooted to the floor. His jaw went slack. Very little in life caught him off guard, but this little pixie managed to surprise him on a daily basis. Shaking off the last vestiges of worry over how she would react, he stood and pulled her into his arms.

"Doll, you never cease to amaze me."

Gail laughed as she wrapped her arms around him. "That's the plan."

"What is?"

"To keep you guessing, of course."

Aidan laughed heartily and was even more encouraged when she joined him.

Eventually, though, Gail brought them back to her original question. "How *do* we capture this guy?"

"*We* don't. The IMB is already coordinating with local police to provide protection. Arrangements are being made—"

Gail shook her head. "Just so you know," she said, "I'm not going to hole up in some house waiting for the Powers-That-Be to put this guy behind bars."

"It may be the only way I can keep you safe."

"I've never played it safe before. Why should I start now?"

Aidan played his ace. "Because I can't stand the thought of you getting hurt."

"Then you keep me safe."

"I can't guarantee—"

"Neither can the police," she countered.

She had a point. So he played his second ace. "I can't focus on finding this guy if I'm busy protecting you."

"Please." She poked him in the ribs. "You are so much better than that."

He brought out the big guns, his third ace. He'd hoped he wouldn't need it, but... "What about the baby?"

She pulled back from him and serious eyes stared into his. "I trust you to take care of all of us, Aidan." She rubbed a hand over her stomach. "Please don't ask us to put our lives on hold because of this criminal." Gail tapped him on the chest. "I have faith in you. In us. We'll catch him."

He pulled her back into his arms and let her spicy scent set his fears aside for the moment. "I know we will, doll."

We have to.

CHAPTER NINETEEN

Aidan awoke with the same heart-pounding fear as the prior morning. Gail wasn't in bed. Noise filtered through to his brain, and adrenaline got overlaid with another, stronger need when his imagination formed a vivid picture of her curves standing under the stream of shower water he heard. His body woke-up fast as he sauntered into the bathroom, ready to play. Aidan couldn't envision ever tiring of her. Each time they came together, he wanted more, wanted to bring both of them to new heights and keep them soaring. Wanted to make sure she felt the same star-exploding climax he did. And over and over again, until neither of them could move. It was a heady feeling and scared the shit out of him at the same time.

That insatiable need replaced the fear he'd woken up with. Good thing he slept naked. Poking his head around the curtain, Aidan was met by a water-filled washrag that made direct contact with his face.

"What the—" he sputtered, wiping ineffectually at the rivulets of water running off his chin.

Gail giggled. "You cannot come in here. I've got to get to work and you will make me late."

Aidan pulled out his best puppy-dog-sad look. "I'm wounded. When have I ever made you late for work?" He used the cover of conversation as an opportunity to step into the shower.

"You know damn well I missed most of yesterday because of you." Her eyes wandered over his body and widened when she saw his arousal.

He smiled and stepped closer.

"Aidan." She gulped. "Really, I have to get to work." She backed up until the shower knobs stopped her.

Another step and he was under the spray. He reached for the bar of soap. "I'll just help you, um, wash up." He grinned. "It'll save time."

Gail rushed into the building with a quick glance over her shoulder. She knew Aidan would watch her until she'd buzzed in and passed the guard desk. Another look while she waited for the elevator showed him still parked in the loading zone outside.

As she hurried from the elevator on the floor that housed Thoralssen Industries, she plowed into a wall of muscle that didn't even utter an "oomph" as it steadied her. She looked up and saw an offensive tackle's neck, topped off by a neutral stare and dark buzz cut.

"Good morning, Miss Grayson. I've been assigned to cover you while you're here today."

Seriously? Gail would have laughed if she wasn't still in a minor state of shock. "You're guarding me?"

"Yes, ma'am."

"While I'm here at work? In a secured building?" She waved at the guard already stationed near the reception desk. "There's security already on site, both here and in the main lobby."

"That's what I was hired to do, ma'am." He looked around. "Now, if you'll follow me. I've already cleared your office." He took a couple steps and waited, as if expecting her to fall into step behind him.

It was a good thing she hadn't stopped for her usual coffee on the way in. She'd have most likely spat it out by now. The whole idea of being safeguarded put a bad taste in her mouth. It stank of being ordered around, and she'd had enough of that with her ex. Gail understood this was a serious situation, but she'd promised Aidan she wouldn't leave the building without him today. She never planned on going back on that promise, so why the watchdog?

"Look," she said, "you seem nice enough, but honestly, I don't need my own private bodyguard. I'm at work, for crying out loud."

"I was hired to provide protection while you are on the job."

"That's ridiculous. Who hired you? Aidan?"

"No, ma'am. Mr. Thoralssen hired me."

"Hawk?" Gail all but screeched the name. "Why would Hawk hire a bodyguard for me?"

"I don't know, ma'am. You'll have to ask him."

"You can just bet I will." Gail huffed past the wall of muscle, intent on having this out with her boss.

"If you would like to speak to Mr. Thoralssen, he's in your office waiting for you, along with his wife."

Without losing step, Gail did an about face and headed for her office, glaring iceballs at anyone who got in her way. Having Aidan shadow her every move had been fine. In fact, his need to protect her had been pretty darn endearing. She hadn't had that in a long time, if ever. Gail paused, realizing she loved him even more for his concern.

And yes, this was a potentially dangerous situation. Gail wasn't stupid. She knew that. But she was not about to become a prisoner in her own office. Been there, done that. Not doing it again. She had a few things to say to her boss about this enforced protection.

Julia didn't give her a chance. As soon as Gail's foot crossed the threshold into her office, Julia spoke, hands up to forestall Gail's tirade. "Don't get mad at Hawk. He's keeping you safe."

"Here?" Gail threw her briefcase on the desk. "This is freaking Fort Knox. Nobody could get in." She advanced on Hawk, and he crossed his arms over his chest as if attempting to appear larger than his normally massive self. Gail walked up to him, wishing for the thousandth time that she'd been born with tall-genes.

She narrowed her eyes as she looked up at him. "I don't need a bodyguard, Hawk. It's a waste of money." She tossed her head at the watchdog standing just inside the door.

"Money well spent, in my opinion."

"There's no reason for him to be here. Please. Get rid of him."

"Has he been rude?"

"Of course not."

"Mean? Inappropriate?"

"Hell, no. He wouldn't dare."

"Then I won't get rid of him. And neither will you."

"You already have enough security to stop an assault force."

He smiled at her. "Again, no."

Gail tried another tack. She forced a smile of her own. "Please."

"Absolutely not."

"Ooooh!" Gail's hands came up as if she wanted to choke Hawk. The problem was, she might—or might not—be able to actually reach his neck. She backed off before she tried and slumped down in the chair behind her desk.

"I don't need a bodyguard," she said again, hating her voice, now reduced to a child's I-don't-wanna whine. Gail knew the man was here for her own good, and because Aidan, Julia, even Hawk cared about her. She knew that. But it still irritated the hell out of her. Why hadn't they just asked her?

Hawk came around the desk and put a hand on her shoulder. "You'd have refused if we'd asked you. You're much too independent to tolerate this willingly."

Julia chimed in. "From everything we've heard, this guy on Aidan's case is pretty darn nasty."

"I can hold my own against nasty," Gail said.

The watchdog coughed and she scowled at him, knowing she was being unreasonable and unable to stop herself. Losing control of her life wasn't something she did well.

"You're five-feet-nothing and the last I knew, your black-belt in karate was, well, non-existent," Hawk said.

"Yeah, so?"

"There's also Aidan."

Her head came up. "What about him?"

Hawk lowered his voice. "How much sleep did he get last night?"

Gail colored, causing Hawk to chuckle.

"I'm not talking about that. I'm talking about after. Did he go to sleep?"

"Umm..." Gail tried to remember. After...well, they'd talked for a while. Wrapped in his arms, she'd felt so peaceful, so happy. She may have drifted to sleep while Aidan still spoke. "I don't know."

"Well, I do." Hawk looked at his wife. "I know what it's like to be as worried as Aidan is. Right now, he's gone back to your place to catch some shut-eye."

That got her attention. "He told me he had some things to do."

"He knew he needed some sleep before he did them. What I'm trying to say here is that he will sleep. Now that he knows you're well-protected here at work."

My God, am I so self-absorbed that I didn't notice? What kind of girlfriend does that make me? Gah! Gail felt like an idiot. Of course Aidan's need to protect her would overshadow any instinct toward self-preservation. And, now that she thought about it, the circles under his eyes *had* seemed more pronounced. Shoulders that already felt heavy all of a sudden slumped farther. Why hadn't she seen it? "I wish he'd told me."

"I'm sure he doesn't want to worry you," Julia said.

Gail's eyes flared with anger. "He ought to know by now not to pull that behind-my-back crap on me." Still, the thought of

him out there trying to find that asshole on very little sleep…
Gail shivered. Maybe she should give this guard thing a try.
Anything was worth making sure Aidan was okay. In all actuality, it did feel pretty nice to have her friends, and Aidan, care so much they wanted to keep her safe. That was another first for her. So maybe she could put up with this, for a little while. Gail glanced over at the bodyguard with reluctant acceptance, then back at Hawk and Julia.

"Fine," she said. "But I don't have to like it."

As the week wore on, the fuse on Gail's patience grew shorter and shorter. She'd tolerated this new schedule for Aidan's sake, chafing the entire time. A big cloud was stuck over their heads, ready to pour on them at any moment, and she wanted to shove it out of the way and get on with their lives. She and Aidan had gone out to dinner, toured around San Diego, and tried to do normal things, but his watchfulness turned what should have been dates into security exercises. And during the day it was un-nerving, having a watchdog in her office while she tried to work. He got breaks because building security relieved him as needed.

She didn't. And she wasn't used to that. She'd gone from living alone—from being able to eat when she wanted, go out when she wanted—to being a couple. Aidan seemed to be getting enough rest. He was certainly his jovial old self and tried to keep them on an even keel. Gail smiled, appreciating how hard he worked at that. She should be doing the same thing, but it wasn't easy. They were supposed to be adjusting to this new life together. A life that would be wonderfully complicated when their baby arrived. Instead, it was like they kept waiting for life to collapse around them. Gail couldn't stop thinking about wanting just five minutes all to herself. A sort of claustrophobia had settled in her soul and if she didn't get a few minutes to herself soon, she'd explode.

Worse, it brought up all the shit she'd tried to forget with her ex. Not something she wanted to be thinking of when she'd rather be enjoying this time with Aidan. They'd talked about it last night. She'd told him how hard this was for her.

He'd pulled her into his arms. "I know, doll. It's not the way I want things, either."

"No, Aidan. You don't understand. She blew out a long breath. "You remember William? My ex?"

"Kind of hard to forget the asshole," Aidan answered, his arms tightening around her.

"Well, the thing I didn't tell you, the reason he said he screwed around on me? It was because I bored him."

"How the hell—"

Gail put a finger over his lips to shush him. "Let me finish. You know why he thought I was boring? Because he wanted me home. All the time. Didn't want me going out with friends, with him, hell, he didn't even really want me to work, but I put my foot down there. So he kind of molded me into boring, right?

"Because of that, I decided I'd never let someone else dictate my comings and goings. I *am* an interesting person." She tapped his chest with her finger.

"I know you are. You don't have to convince me."

"Yeah, but I feel like I'm right back in that prison."

"Ouch." The pained look on Aidan's face as he pulled away from her proved she'd said the wrong thing once again.

Gail cupped his face in her hands as she tried to make him understand. "I'm not saying you're like him. God, no. You'll never be like him. This enforced protection is bringing up a lot of old crap I thought I'd dealt with. I need some *me* time, Aidan. I know that sounds selfish and it has nothing to do with wanting to be with you. It has to do with me needing to make at least some of my own decisions here."

He'd sympathized, then told her it hopefully wouldn't be much longer. "I can't take a chance, Gail. I can't give him any opportunity to get to you. Do you understand that?"

In the end, she'd capitulated, knowing his peace of mind was more important than hers at the moment. But it bit. Big time. The only time she seemed to get to herself now was in the bathroom. And even then, her guard had to "clear the room" before she could use it. He'd been adamant about that. Talk about Neanderthal. The only reason she was still putting up with it all was that it made life easier for Aidan.

Still, she was pretty much down to her last nerve. Worse, it felt like the walls were closing in on her. She'd always loved this office, but it felt too small with her and the bodyguard sharing space. She couldn't get enough air in her lungs, couldn't concentrate.

And Aidan's warning to her watchdog this morning pretty much validated her mood. At least, she thought it was a warning. When she'd questioned the guard, he'd been closed-mouthed about the whole thing. And Aidan hadn't explained what they'd talked about when she spoke to him on the phone a while ago. No amount of cajoling worked.

So now here she sat. In prison. At work. Unable to focus on anything but how much she needed to remember who Gail Grayson was before she lost herself. Some time to think without feeling like she was behind a glass bubble and being watched. Some time all to herself. *Alone.*

Knowing it wasn't a good idea, but unable to get past the growing need for a few minutes of alone time, Gail began to plot ways to make that happen. Aidan looked more rested, a huge relief. Maybe he could relieve her prison guard for a day and she could visit a spa. No way she'd take her watchdog to a salon. Aidan probably wouldn't let her go alone, either.

So it would have to be something here. Something at work so Aidan wouldn't worry overmuch. Just ten minutes to herself somewhere other than a bathroom. That's all she wanted. Gail toyed with the empty teacup on her desk. Boy, what she wouldn't give to curl up with a good book and a hot cup of tea.

When the idea came to her, she nodded so emphatically that the guard looked up from his magazine. "Everything all right, Miss Grayson?"

It even pissed her off that he'd kept the formalities, even though she'd tried several times to get him to call her Gail. Hell, she didn't even know if he was a Jim, or Tom, or Mike. He was just Stomson. That was what the watchdog went by. The man was an automaton. "Yes. Just fine. Sorry, I reacted to an idea I came up with...for a campaign slogan."

He stared at her for a long moment and she worked hard to keep her eyes normal, her lips quirked in a friendly little smile. An innocent look. If she couldn't beat 'em, she'd have to find a way for them to join her. Aidan would be pissed, but hopefully not too bad.

Gail waited a full hour before stretching and staring into her tea mug. "Stomson?"

"Yes, Ms. Grayson?"

"How about we take a short walk? There's a small bookstore around the corner. I'd like to pick up a couple books."

"What titles? I'll have them ordered for you." Her guard reached for his phone.

"No," she said, a little too fast. "I need to stretch my legs. The place is like ten steps away from the front door. I need to stare at something other than work and home, just for a little while."

"Not a smart thing to do right now."

"Please?" God, Gail hated begging.

When he still looked unconvinced, she let some consternation out, just for show. "It's only two doors down, for crying out loud. How can anyone get to me with you right by my side?"

He eyed her as if assessing whether or not she told the truth. When he blew out a breath, the only emotion the man had shown since she'd known him, Gail knew he'd do it.

"This isn't a good idea, you know," he said.

She couldn't help letting just a bit of snarky out. "Seriously, do you doubt your ability to protect me that much?"

When he frowned, she quickly backpedaled. "I know you've got my safety front and center in your mind. I appreciate that. I'm just...well, I'm feeling closed in. I need some different air for a few minutes. I promise. No more than ten minutes inside the bookstore."

With his lips in tight lines, her watchdog checked the hall, motioning her to follow him. Once in the lobby, his head moved from side to side as his sharp eyes surveyed the area. At the door, he held out a hand to stop her.

"Again, this is not a good idea. You know that, right?"

Gail held her head high. "Maybe not, but it's better than climbing the walls of my office."

"Fine. You do exactly as I tell you. You don't follow one order and I'll haul you back here over my shoulder. Got it?"

"Got it," Gail said, trying to keep from laughing. He could try.

"Stay beside the building. I'll walk street-side. Once at the bookstore, we both go in, I clear it, then you get ten minutes."

Yes!

"Where I can see you at all times," he finished.

Damn. Well, at least it was something different to look at. Gail nodded.

Freedom smelled like car fumes and humid sunshine and it was a heavenly scent. She soaked it up, taking deep breaths. Focused on this minor freedom, she didn't hear the screech of brakes.

Or see the side door open on the black van. When she turned at some commotion, she found Stomson in the fight of his life. Three masked men pummeled him. He fought valiantly but was outmatched. Gail knew he'd lose.

And it was all her fault.

She felt the sting of a needle just as a fourth person yanked her inside the van. Gail instantly regretted ever talking her watchdog into this outing. He'd been right.

As her vision faded, she saw ski-mask covered heads and heard the pounding on the outside of the van as it roared away.

She'd been taken.

And she had played right into their hands.

I'm so sorry, Aidan.

Then everything faded to black.

CHAPTER TWENTY

When Aidan arrived at Hawk's office, he didn't stop at the door, didn't break stride. He walked right up to the bloodied-but-still-standing bodyguard and cold-cocked him with a right hook. Aidan was a good-sized guy and he worked out enough to pack a pretty decent punch. But this guy took the hit without flinching or moving, except for turning his head sideways to deflect some of the blow.

Aidan pulled his arm back and tried again. The man met his fist halfway and stopped it in mid-air. He leaned toward Aidan. "The one, you get free. I owe you that. This one, though, is going to cost you. You willing to pay that price?"

"Yes, goddammit!"

"No," Hawk said, coming up beside them. "He's not. At least, I'm not." He put a hand on Aidan's shoulder. "This does not help us find Gail."

Aidan glared at the man a moment longer before relenting. He dropped his arm briefly, then brought it back up in a flash. His fist whizzed by the bodyguard before the man could react.

Aidan never touched him, never planned to. Instead, paint and sheet rock gave way to the onslaught of his fury and a gaping wound was left in the wall. It didn't help assuage his fear, his anger.

Gail had been taken. And just like that, the last chink in his armor was gone. His entire world both fell into place and shattered into a million pieces all at the same time.

He loved her. Oh, God, he loved her.

She was his life and now her own life could very well be in danger. A dozen images flew through his brain. Ops he'd been on. Blood he'd seen shed, all to satisfy someone's sick greed or need for power.

Aidan walked stiffly over to stare out the window. It would never be enough for those people. There was always more that needed to be owned, to be subjugated. Salvena thought he was better than all of them. The funny thing was, he was no different than the last criminal they'd gone after. And he was the same as the next one would be.

It all seemed so damn futile, this struggle between the good guys and the bad. And now, the person he cherished above all else was in mortal danger.

"Here's Detective Smith," Hawk said. "Let's start by seeing what he's got."

Aidan remained with his back to them all, but his ears were tuned to any new information.

"Not much, I'm afraid. As your bodyguard mentioned, a black GMC van pulled up as Ms. Grayson raced down the sidewalk. Two hooded men jumped out—"

Aidan flinched.

"—and pulled her into the van. There were no plates, front or back. No bumper stickers to ID the van, nothing. It went down so fast, we don't even have any eye witnesses, except for the bodyguard. It stinks of a professional hit."

"Tell us something we don't know," Aidan muttered.

"There's not much more we can tell you, except that her apartment appears untouched."

Aidan turned around, his fists clenched. "You went to her apartment?"

"As soon as Mr. Thoralssen contacted us, yes. It was a slim chance at best, but sometimes, it can pay off. So we checked out her place. This time, however..." The detective shrugged, his meaning clear.

That would mean they saw the surprise he'd set up that was for Gail's eyes only. The surprise he might never... No. He cut the thought off mid-stride. That kind of thought was how you got killed.

"The way she was taken has all the appearance of a kidnapping. Does Ms. Grayson have any family? Who would a kidnapper call to make demands?" The detective looked at Hawk, but the answer came from Aidan.

"Me."

Detective Smith turned to Aidan. "Then we need to set up surveillance and phone taps."

"No."

"It's standard in these situations. We might be able to trace the call," the detective said.

"You won't. Salvena's too smart."

"Salvena?"

"A Colombian drug lord who has an issue with Aidan."

The detective's eyes widened as he stared at Hawk. "What kind of issue?"

"An 'I killed his son' kind of issue." Aidan voice turned calm and cold. He wasn't Aidan Walker anymore. He was any one of a number of nefarious aliases. Undercover work meant hiding the truth, so he'd learned to bury it all, compartmentalize it to the far regions of his brain. He did that now. Buried the fear, the hatred, even the love. It was the only way he could find her. And it was the hardest thing he'd ever done.

Smith stared at Aidan for a long moment, then flipped his notebook closed. "I can see this is bigger than a kidnapping."

That buried emotion wanted to pummel the officer, make him understand nothing was more important than finding Gail. Instead, Aidan remained silent, shoving his fists in his jeans pockets to keep from doing something he'd regret.

The detective continued speaking. "I'm going to get the drug guys over here to help figure out the next move."

"They don't have to figure out anything," Aidan said to Hawk. "Salvena's got it all worked out already. It's all about making me pay. He'll sweat me first, call somewhere in the twelve-to-twenty-four-hour time frame. He's already scoped out where we'll meet. How I'll make my entrance. Where he'll place his men for protection. Everything's been finely tuned. That's why he didn't make a move when he first entered the country."

"That makes sense," Hawk said, placing a hand on Aidan's shoulder.

Aidan didn't budge, didn't show surprise at the contact, even though he wanted to shake Hawk's hand off and race out to search blindly for Gail.

"So, no taps?" Hawk said.

"No." Aidan held the taller man's gaze for a long moment, never wavering.

"All right," Hawk said, deciding. He turned to the officer. "Thank you for the help, officer. I'd like the name of the captain who runs your drug enforcement team. I'll call him and apprise him of the situation."

"You can't just shut down an investigation," Detective Smith said.

"We're not shutting it down, just...elevating it," Hawk said.

Aidan saw Hawk glance at Julia, who picked up her phone and slipped out of the room.

"Sorry, detective," Hawk said. "No offense meant."

"None taken. I worked the drug beat for a while. Went back to straight police work. Figured it was safer." He jotted something down in his notebook, ripped the page off and handed it to Hawk, jerking his head toward Aidan. "Just make certain you don't let him go off half-cocked to get his girlfriend back, you hear? Be sure you call the captain. I'll check in with him later."

"We will," Hawk said, leading the officer to the door. "Thank you, both for your quick response and for your discretion."

"No problem. I know about Thoralssen Industries. Know what it used to be, and what it is now." Detective Smith shook Hawk's hand. "You do a lot of good, here and across the world."

Hawk canted his head briefly in acknowledgement. "We try."

"Keep up the good work."

Once Detective Smith left and only Aidan remained, Hawk pulled the cord out that held his hair in a short tail and ran his fingers through the strands. "This really bites."

"Yeah," Aidan said. "Thanks for getting rid of the cop."

"It was pretty obvious that he wouldn't be able to help us."

Aidan nodded at the door to Julia's office. "She calling for reinforcements?"

"Yes."

"Good."

Hawk nodded. "What say, when she's done, we move this op to our house? At least we can be comfortable while we wait."

"I won't be comfortable until Gail's safely home."

Hawk clapped Aidan on the shoulder again, his grip digging in. "None of us will."

CHAPTER TWENTY-ONE

The fog lifted slowly from Gail's muddled mind. At first, she thought she'd taken a mid-morning nap. Tiredness had taken on new meaning nowadays. Except this didn't feel like her lumpy bed. The mattress was firm, but comfortable. The room was warm and smelled of...lavender? Gail opened her eyes and glanced around.

She had no clue where she was. And her neck ached. She touched the spot and then shot off the bed when everything came flooding back. A wave of dizziness stilled her and she clutched her stomach, praying whatever they'd injected her with hadn't hurt the baby. Gail had to wait for the dizziness to subside before she could even begin to figure out where the hell she was and who had taken her.

Aidan! He'd come for her, take any chance necessary to find her. Oh, man, she'd really mucked things up this time. This was all her fault and if Aidan got hurt...

Gail couldn't let that happen. She got up slowly, glad when the dizziness didn't return. The room was set up like a hotel room. A very plush hotel room. In San Diego? There could only be a couple hotels that fit the bill for this level of luxury.

She walked over to the window and glanced outside. Yep. She was at the Destiny, an upscale hotel in an amazingly secluded area on the outskirts of town, known for its discretion. She'd always wanted to stay here, but it was way outside her price range.

Why was she here now? And how much danger was she in? Gail picked up the phone. Dead. Of course. And no purse, so no cell phone.

There were three doors. One led to a bathroom bigger than her apartment. Another, which probably led to the hall, was locked. Gail couldn't figure out how they could lock a hotel room from the outside. Before she could check the last door, a wave of nausea hit her and she rushed for the bathroom.

When she came out, Gail froze. She was no longer alone. A dark man sat in one of the chairs by the window, and some goon stood by the door.

"Good evening, Miss Grayson. I trust you are well?"

"As well as one can be after being abducted," she spat. "Let me go."

"I cannot do that. Not until I have what I came for. Come and sit."

"No, thank you."

The very large, very mean-looking goon by the door headed her way, so rather than be manhandled, Gail took the chair opposite the man, maintaining a stiff posture.

"I'm sure you will be relieved to know that the tranquilizer we used on you will not harm your baby."

Gail's eyes widened. "How do you know?"

"My men found telltale signs at your apartment."

She hated that they'd been in her place, but the relief that her baby wouldn't be harmed took precedence over everything else. Gail sat back, resting a hand on her stomach. "So you're the drug-seller."

He squinted briefly before hiding behind a smile. "I do what I must for my family."

"The family who died."

She had a moment's guilt at the quick show of grief on his face. Then Salvena covered it and jumped up. In one step, he was at her chair, pinning her arms to the cushion with his hands. "You do not have the right to mention my son to me, Miss Grayson. I may not want to harm your baby, but I'm not above teaching you a lesson or two."

Gail stared him down, quaking like a fucking leaf internally, until he backed off. Salvena stretched his neck from side to side. "Mr. Walker chose his partner well. You've as much fire in your belly as he does. Well, not for long. You see, Miss Grayson,

Aidan took the one thing most precious to me. He stole my son. And I, in turn, will steal his progeny."

What? Gail couldn't comprehend, tried to understand what the man had just said. But the words oozed through her brain like green goo until one word settled in her heart. *Progeny.*

"You're going to kill my baby?"

"No," he said. "I am not the animal your Walker is. I will raise your baby as my own. He can't replace—"

A roaring in her ears drowned out what Salvena said. Gail tried to stem the ice-cold panic that froze her body into immobility. They wanted to take her baby? Her heart pounded a harsh rhythm as the panic threatened to engulf her. No way. No *fucking* way he would get her baby. She should do something, attack him, something to make him take back those words. Her brain shut down as the dread dripped in like the frozen needles of frostbite.

"You will never get near my child. Never."

Salvena laughed. "You will have no choice in the matter. Once I get you to my home, there will be no chance of escape. You will spend your confinement under my watchful eye. After the baby is born...well, we'll see what happens. Maybe I will give you to my men."

He trailed a finger along her cheek and Gail yanked her head back, away from his touch.

"You do have a certain cuteness to you. My men like their women feisty." Still chuckling, Salvena strode out of the room, his goon behind him. The unmistakable sound of a lock meant there would be no escape through the third and final door in her room. Gail gulped, recognizing that her own bravado might well get her killed. No, Salvena wouldn't kill her. He wanted her alive, at least until she gave birth. Then...

He would *never* get her child. Aidan's child. *Never.* Gail fought the panic and tried to think.

On shaky legs, she walked to the door Salvena and his goon had left through and leaned her head against it, both arms hugging her stomach. She heard murmured words, but could only make out a few of them. Spanish wasn't a language she interpreted easily, especially with her mind whirling around Salvena's plan.

How could she fight this man and protect her baby?

Aidan would come for her. She knew that like her own breath. Because of her foolishness, because she'd wanted an ounce of her freedom back, she'd endangered her baby, and the man she loved might well be killed in the process of rescuing her.

What had she done?

CHAPTER TWENTY-TWO

The afternoon crawled by as Aidan waited for Salvena to call. The only thing keeping him sane was the unwavering belief that his enemy would not harm Gail or the baby. No, he'd want to hurt Aidan, either by killing him slowly in front of Gail, letting Aidan see her pain, or... Aidan gulped. He refused to think of the alternative.

Hawk's wife had tried to get him to eat, but he had no stomach for it. Instead, he paced. Then sat. Then paced some more.

The doorbell rang. Aidan barely heard it as Hawk answered it. But when Dion walked in, carrying little Joseph, Aidan blinked and stood. How the hell had he gotten here?

Claire, Dion's wife, rushed right past her husband and threw her arms around Aidan. "You'll find her," she said. "I know you will. Especially with Dion and Hawk working with you."

He tried to set her away, but she wouldn't let go. She held on as if he were her lifeline. In moments, he realized the opposite was true. She'd offered him a lifeline. Slowly, Aidan hugged Claire back. Still holding back emotion, he couldn't help the long, wracking sigh he let loose into her shoulder.

"Good," she said, backing up. "Now you can focus." Claire took little Joseph from Dion and whispered in his ear. He touched her cheek before she left the room with the baby.

"We know where Salvena is holding up," Dion said.

"What? You couldn't lead with that?"

"My wife said no business until she knew you were okay."

"Where is he? And how the hell did you find him?"

"Ecker called in some favors."

God bless Director Ecker. He'd given them hell through the years, but Aidan's boss always backed them up one hundred percent. And always had their back.

"So, where?" Aidan asked again.

"A hotel on the outskirts of the city."

He checked the gun he'd gone through a hundred times already today. "Let's go," he said.

Then his cell rang.

Aidan, Dion, and Hawk all stared at it. On the third ring, Aidan snapped out of it and answered his phone. "Where is she, you asshole?"

"She is safe, as is your unborn child."

A miniscule bit of relief seeped its way into Aidan's heart.

"But, she will not be for long if you do not do as I say."

Aidan remained quiet.

"Be in front of the *Midway* in one hour. A van will pick you up. If you are not there, your future dies, just as mine did when you murdered my son."

It took everything he had not to argue with the man. "I'll be there."

Aidan disconnected the phone and turned to Dion and Hawk. "The carrier, on the Embarcadero. One hour."

"Okay," Dion said. "I called the captain on the way here. They're staking out the hotel and gathering as much intel as they can. I'll have him send some men..."

"No." Aidan slashed his hand through the air. "I know this man. He won't take me anywhere there's a chance I can see Gail. Not at first. He wants me to suffer." Aidan winced. He had already suffered more than he'd thought it possible for one human to endure. His heart had been sliced into a million tiny pieces. "He'll take me somewhere else."

"Then we'll follow you."

"He'll see you."

"No, he won't. We're good. You know that." The fierceness in Dion's eyes must have been mirrored in his own. They'd been through enough ops together that Aidan could finish Dion's sentences, and vice versa. Dion was the only one Aidan would trust with this. Hawk too, since he looked about ready to tear something to bits.

"I know you're that good," Aidan said quietly. "But I need you focused on Gail. I'm the distraction. I'll keep Salvena's eyes, mind, and black heart on me so you can get to Gail."

Dion clapped his hand on Aidan's shoulder and stared at him. Aidan knew that his ex-partner understood what being the distraction would mean to Aidan in terms of pain. But he didn't say it. Instead, he gripped Aidan's shoulder tight for a moment, then released it. "Okay," Dion said. "What's the plan?"

After ten minutes of hasty preparation, Aidan borrowed Hawk's Harley and headed for the meet. His head was focused on rescuing Gail, but his heart wanted to plan all the things he would do to Salvena once Gail was safe. This was it. The rest of his life depended on what would happen in the next few hours. If Gail didn't...

No. He froze the thought. She would be safe. Dion was the best there was at this. Between him and Hawk, they would make certain Gail was safe. They had to. There was no other option.

Aidan parked the bike and sat observing the area around the aircraft carrier. Tours were closed for the evening, but this was the Embarcadero. People milled about and walked along the sidewalk, a mixture of locals and tourists. Nothing seemed amiss.

When there were only five minutes left until the meet time, Aidan walked across the street and leaned against a railing, looking decidedly more relaxed than he felt. It didn't take long for the van to roll up, and it appeared to be the same one that nabbed Gail.

The side door opened and Aidan didn't hesitate. He grabbed the door and climbed in, was manhandled to the ground, and absorbed the few punches they tossed his way while they tied his arms behind his back and a black bag was thrown over his head. He could see a bit of light through the material, but nothing distinct.

After several minutes of turns and twists Aidan tried to memorize, the van slowed and everything got darker. Had they driven into a building or garage?

When the van stopped, the door slid open almost immediately. Then he was roughly yanked out and pushed forward until he fell to his knees in what appeared to be an empty warehouse.

Two brutes pulled him up and dragged him across a rough concrete floor. They tossed him onto a wooden chair, retying his arms behind it and tying his ankles to the legs of the chair. Aidan squirmed, testing for weaknesses and found none.

He was a sitting duck, just waiting for whatever Salvena wanted to throw at him. He thought of Gail, of their baby, and let the love wash over him, calm him. Dion and Hawk would get to them. He believed it with everything he knew and felt. What happened to him wasn't important. The only thing that mattered was Gail and the baby.

Darkness, because of the bag, made it difficult for Aidan to tell how much time passed. He heard shuffling, and once in a while someone slapped him or even punched him in the gut, or face. Just enough to remind him he had one hell of a beating coming.

Like he didn't already know that?

After what felt like thirty or so minutes but could have been an hour or two, a light flashed on in front of him and the bag was ripped off his head.

Aidan squinted, acclimating to the brightness that shone directly at him.

"So," a familiar voice said from behind the light. "You are finally mine to deal with as I've been waiting for, planning for."

Aidan cocked his head, affecting a comfort he didn't feel. "Took you long enough. I figured you'd have me days ago."

"Ah, but these things are not to be rushed. There were plans to organize so that there would be no interruption this time. And so I could learn about and acquire that which is most precious to you."

Aidan's façade slipped momentarily. "Where is she, you bastard? I want eyes on her before we go any further. I want to see that she is unharmed. And if she isn't..." He let the words trail off. They both knew what Aidan would do to Salvena if he got the chance.

"You do not have much bargaining power, Mr. Aidan Walker. You have a lot of arrogance, but it is inconsequential. You cannot move, cannot escape. You are mine to do with as I please. As are your woman and your unborn child."

Fuck. Salvena wouldn't harm a pregnant woman, would he? Aidan prayed knowledge of the baby would keep him from hurting Gail, at least for a while.

"Don't worry about the mother and baby. Both are fine and being held in...relative comfort."

"You've got what you want. Me." Aidan tried the standard plea. "Let her go."

Salvena moved in front of the light so Aidan could see him. The man was as dark and swarthy as the pirates of old. His eyes were black beads in a face that had aged since Aidan last saw him.

"Miss Grayson will not be released, at least not anytime soon. You see, I have plans for her."

"Whatever you do to her, you bastard, I'll do to you tenfold when I get my hands on you."

"That will never happen. You see, you will die a slow, lingering, painful death, while your woman and her unborn child will come with me. Though he or she will not replace my dear son whom I loved, I will raise your child as my own."

Shock hit Aidan at the same time as the fist blindsided him, and his head whipped back from the force of the blow that sent an arc of blood flying. He didn't feel the pain, only rage at Salvena's words. With renewed fury, Aidan fought the bonds that held him, struggled to get to the man, even managed to raise his chair off the ground until a kidney punch knocked the wind out of him and he slumped back down.

"You bastard."

"Your child is the bastard," Salvena said with a deadly chuckle. "But not for long. And you…you will die knowing your son or daughter will be raised to work in the occupation you abhor. The profession you've spent your life fighting against. Yes, he or she will thrive, and will never know the righteousness of their biological father."

Salvena waved his hand and a fist hit him again. And again. And again. Before long, pain was all Aidan could feel. Every bit of him hurt. One eye was bloodied and swollen shut, the other one no more than a slit. Yet he could see Salvena smiling placidly as his men worked Aidan over.

Way beyond the pain now, he kept his focus on the man he knew he would kill, as the beating continued.

CHAPTER TWENTY-THREE

Dion and Hawk met the captain and S.W.A.T. teams a block from the hotel. The captain had floorplans spread out on the hood of his car. Between the intel they'd gotten from Ecker and the local information about the hotel, it didn't take long to format a plan. They'd narrowed the rooms Gail could be in down to two, thankfully back-to-back.

Dion tugged at the waiter's uniform he'd commandeered for his use. It might be cliché but it surprised him how often waiters were overlooked. Hopefully, that rule would hold true again today.

Hawk stood beside Dion looking decidedly unhappy. "There's got to be something I can do."

"You're a civilian, Hawk," Dion said, trying to straighten his bow tie.

"So are you."

"I've got a resume."

"So do I."

"Yeah, for piracy."

They both chuckled, but it was forced. Tension mounted, waiting for the go on the op. This was life or death. Dion had been there before, but never when he'd had so much to lose. He thought of Claire and little Joseph. They were his life, and the reason he didn't do this type of work anymore. He wanted to grow old with them.

Dion shook his head. Sentiment didn't play well when you were about to kick some ass. He tucked a gun into the back of his waistband and straightened the tux jacket over the bulge.

"You will be helping," Dion said, tucking an earwig in his ear. "You'll have my back from command." He waved at the mobile unit behind them, handing Hawk a walkie-talkie. "I can't have eyes everywhere."

"I don't like it. I should be helping more. But I'll do it."

Hawk's size was impressive, and Dion thought again about partnering with him. But he didn't have time to train him. No, they'd have to go in covert and with just a small contingent.

"Time to go," the captain said, walking up to them.

Hawk clapped Dion on the shoulder. "Be safe."

Dion nodded, his head already walking through the memorized floorplan.

He was the forward man. He'd walk the hall, delivering room service food, and disable the man outside the rooms. The problem was, the camera on that floor had a blind spot. They couldn't tell how many men were in the hallway.

The elevator dinged and Dion stepped off, turned and headed down the hall. As he turned the corner, he saw only one guard. He coughed, the signal to Hawk and the captain's men that there was only one guard.

It should have been easy, but the two rooms were at the very end of the hall and the guard was savvy.

"Stop." The guard kept Dion from rolling the cart to the end room. "No room service was ordered."

"Sir, I have a request from that room"—he pointed to the door across the hall and slightly down from the guard— "for caviar and champagne." Dion wiggled the bottle in the bucket of ice.

"Deliver it later. You need to leave. Now."

"If I don't deliver this"—he messed with the champagne again— "my manager will write me up. Look." Dion held up the slip of paper. "See the order?"

The guard took one step closer and it was just enough for Dion to make his move. He yanked the champagne bottle out and caught the guard on the side of the head with a sickening thud. The big man slumped to the floor unconscious and without a single sound to alert anyone indoors.

At least, that's what he hoped.

Salvena hadn't returned to Gail's room. That should have relieved her, but instead, it worried the hell out of her. If he wasn't here, where was he? And where was Aidan? He would do whatever he must to save her, and that worried her more than anything.

She wandered around the room for the hundredth time, searching for any way to escape. The thud, when she heard it, was against the outside wall. It was subtle, but something had definitely hit the wall. The door between the adjoining rooms began to open and Gail grabbed the light off the table, brandishing it like a baseball bat.

As soon as the person came into view, she swung.

Only quick reflexes saved the man from being cold-cocked. He grabbed the lamp and moved with it, hitting the door with a *thunk*.

"Holy hell!" he said.

Gail didn't wait for him to regroup. She raced past him and was almost out the door before his words stopped her cold.

"Gail. Stop. It's me, Dion."

She whirled around, her hand holding the door open. The goon she'd seen before lay in a heap on the floor. When she raised her eyes, it was to the relieved amber gaze of Dion Gaetani.

Relief flooded her and Dion moved quickly to her side, helping her to the bed when she started to shake.

"We've got her," he said to someone she couldn't see. "The coast is clear."

"No," Gail said. "It's not. Where's Aidan? Salvena hasn't been here for a couple hours. If Aidan's not here, then he's in danger. I know he is."

Dion took Gail's hand as police filed in and handcuffed the slowly waking goon. "He went to meet with Salvena."

"Oooh, no! He'll kill him. Dion, Salvena will kill Aidan. We have to—"

"I know," Dion said, his voice calm. "We weren't able to follow him, but that doesn't mean we can't track him." He tapped his earwig. "How's the signal?"

"What do you mean, signal?" Gail asked. "Why are we waiting? We have to find him."

Dion held up his hand, listening. After a couple seconds, he nodded and looked at Gail. "It looks like Aidan was right. They didn't bring him here."

"How do you—"

"The plan was for Aidan to get an active tracker stuck to the van. We have a position."

He led Gail out of the room, but she made it to the elevator before him. She had to get to Aidan. If anything happened to him— Gail clutched her stomach.

On the ride down, Dion told her he'd have someone take her to Hawk and Julia's.

"No way," she said. "I'm going with you."

"You can't."

"Try me," she said, fisting her hands.

"Aidan said you'd want to and that I was, under no circumstances, to allow that." Dion lowered his voice. "We can rescue him, but he has to know you're safe."

"I'll stay back. Really I will. Have someone stay with me. But I *have* to be there. I love him, Dion. I have to go."

The elevator doors opened and Gail blocked the door, biting her lower lip as he regarded her. Finally, he gave a curt nod. "All right. But you stay where I tell you to, and you do exactly as I say."

Interminable minutes passed as they made their way by another van to the warehouse area from which Aidan's tracker pinged. Though it about killed Gail, she stayed in the op truck with an officer who'd been threatened with dire circumstances if he let her out.

"I guess we're both considered civilians," Hawk said, standing by her side.

Gail didn't reply. Instead, she watched as Dion, with only two other men, crept toward the warehouse. Before long, they'd disappeared inside, and all she could do was wait, since her guard had apparently taken Dion's threat to heart and stood barring the door.

Silent minutes passed. Minutes that seemed like hours. Hawk put his arm around her and Gail held on as if she'd drown without his support.

She held on and prayed.

Pfft. Pfft. Pfft.

Gunfire? Gail moaned and would have slumped to the floor without Hawk's steadying arm. She couldn't hear anything over the pounding of her heart. It reverberated against her eardrums. Nothing moved, nothing mattered. Her entire world would disintegrate if any of those bullets had hit their mark. Gail's hand covered her mouth and unshed tears blurred her vision.

Still they waited. She watched the clock. Seconds ticked by, then the minute hand slowly moved. One minute, two, three. Hanging by a thread, she barely breathed as they waited.

An officer put a hand over the earphones he wore, listening. Finally, he spoke. "They got him!"

"Who?" Gail and Hawk asked at the same time.

"Walker. It's okay, miss. He's safe." The officer patted her shoulder. "It's over."

Gail gasped in great gulps of air, filling her lungs as she bent over. When she straightened, she took a step toward the door guard.

"I'm going out there."

"I can't let you do that," he said.

Hawk stepped to her side, standing impressively tall in the small truck. "Yes, you can. I know you're doing your job." Hawk glanced at the officer's hand. "Would your wife be satisfied to stay in here if that were you outside?"

The officer gulped and shook his head, then moved aside.

Gail was out the door and racing toward the warehouse as Dion came out with a bloody and bedraggled Aidan at his side. When he saw her, his smile lit up a face nearly unrecognizable.

Gail leaped into his arms and Aidan grunted but held on tight, burying his head in her neck. Tears flowed freely and she couldn't let go, kept touching him everywhere, afraid that he was a mirage, a happy fantasy to blur a reality she didn't want to know.

When she finally backed up, she realized she'd been squeezing an injured man very tightly. "I'm so sorry. Did I hurt you?"

Aidan pulled her back into his tight embrace. "Nothing matters but you. You could never hurt me, unless you leave me."

Gail tried to laugh, but it came out kind of like a hysterical hiccup. Which, of course, made her laugh more.

It took long moments to control the gasping hiccups so she could answer. She pulled back and tucked herself under Aidan's arm, shaking her head. "Never leaving you, bud. And don't think you can get rid of me, either. I'm here for the long haul."

He hugged her tight to his side. "Me, too, love. Me, too."

"If you two are done going all googly-eyed over each other," Dion cut in, "do you think maybe we can get this man to a hospital?"

"I don't need a hospital," Aidan said.

"Yes," the captain said as he walked up. "You do."

CHAPTER TWENTY-FOUR

Gail hadn't left his side and Aidan felt sap-happy over it. He needed her there as he fought to let go of the final vestiges of worry and fear.

The doctors wanted him to stay the night. No way. X-rays didn't show any broken bones except for a finger they taped. Granted, he probably looked horrible and had needed some stitches, but he wasn't staying in the hospital.

So after some work convincing the doctors, and a few signed forms, Gail helped him get dressed and they walked out arm in arm. Well, arm under arm, since she insisted she help "support" him in his weakened state. Aidan decided that as soon as they got back to her place, he'd show her just how weak he wasn't.

Seeing Dion and Claire waiting outside almost made him groan. He was tired of being poked and prodded and wanted Gail all to himself for a while. Hell, for forever.

"Come on," Claire said, pulling them toward the SUV they'd rented while in town. "We're all meeting at Hawk and Julia's to decompress."

Aidan didn't want to decompress, damn it. He wanted to go home. With Gail. And press the matter of their relationship.

Gail laughed as Claire nudged them toward the back seat, and Aidan tried to bury his irritation. She'd earned some fun, some laughter. More than earned it. Their relationship had started off pretty rocky, but Aidan vowed to show her what a boring, urban counterpart he could be. Husband. He'd been mulling that word over for a while now and it was time to act on it.

At Hawk's place, Julia clasped Gail's arms, then hugged her. "I don't know what I'd do if I lost you."

Aidan extracted Gail from Julia's arms. "She's safe, so no more tears."

Julia swiped at her eyes.

"I'm okay, too, by the way," Aidan said, making them all laugh.

Julia hugged him, too, then suggested they all sit. She'd filled the nervous hours by baking and preparing food and everything was just about ready.

Claire followed Julia into the kitchen after they each refused Gail's help. Hawk indicated a chair on deck for Gail to sit in, but when Aidan settled on the settee, she joined him there, snuggling into him with no apparent care for anyone else.

It puffed Aidan's chest up. She loved him. He knew it. He loved her, too. He just needed the right moment to tell her.

Salvena had done one good thing. He'd given Aidan clarity, helped him figure out what he wanted. He wanted it all. Marriage, kids—hell, even the white picket fence if that's what she wanted. She'd gone to bat for him. Dion had pulled him aside to tell him that. Gail Grayson was his life. His ever after. And he never wanted her to leave his side.

Aidan watched as Julia set down a tray of drinks and she and Claire joined their husbands. There was a lot of love in this home right now.

First, Dion had found Claire. Of course, Aidan had just about had to hit his friend over the head to get him to realize it. Now married, they had little Joseph, and judging by how they still gazed into each other's eyes, another one would be on the way shortly.

Even Hawk had found his happily ever after, with Julia. Two more perfectly matched people, Aidan had never seen.

Aidan and Gail weren't exactly a perfect match. Aidan figured their life would be filled with fights...and kissing and making up. He smiled. He could live with that. Couldn't live without it, for that matter.

At that moment, a lot of happiness surrounded their burgeoning love. Maybe it was time to make it official. Granted, Gail was still coming down off the adrenaline rush of being kidnapped, rescued, and having the love of her life beaten almost within an inch of his. He grimaced as a sore rib poked him. He must look like hell.

The idea popped into his head like a phone call in the middle of the night. Would it work? It had to.

"Ouch!"

"Sorry," he whispered in Gail's ear. "Did I hurt you?"

"Not much, but you were hugging me pretty hard." She eyed him closely. "What were you thinking about?"

"Nothing."

He tried to turn away, but she held him in place with a finger to his cheek.

"It wasn't nothing."

"No," he said. "It wasn't nothing." He extricated himself from her arms, making her frown.

She kept frowning, right up until he knelt on one knee in front of her, with a feminine screech from Julia and an "about time" from Claire as the backdrop.

"I love you," Aidan said, then placed a hand on her belly. "And I love this new little life we've created."

Gail stared at him, wide-eyed.

"I know I had a hard time getting used to it. Blame it on my background and my own stubborn, muddled head. I thought I'd put it all behind me, but apparently, some of that luggage got lost, only to resurface at the worst of times. Gail..."

Her expectant gaze almost undid him.

"I want this baby. I want to love this baby. I know I'm a screw-up."

Julia harrumphed behind him and Aidan turned to glare at her.

"I know I haven't done right by you, Gail," he continued. "But I want to."

"For the baby?" she asked.

"Yes."

When her eyes shadowed, Aidan wondered what the hell he'd said that got her guard up. Then he realized his mistake.

"For the baby," he reiterated. "And for you. And for me. I can't imagine life without you...either of you. I love you both, and I've only met one of you. How can that be?" He didn't understand it, but knew it to be the truth.

The shadows disappeared from Gail's eyes and she smiled. "Because that's what love is. Sight unseen, it fills your heart until there's nothing else you can think about. That's how I think of you," she said.

"And I think about you. So... what do you say?"

"About what?"

"Oh, come on. Are you going to make me actually ask?"

"Yes!" all three women answered at the same time. Even Dion and Hawk chimed in with their chuckles.

"Just get it over with," Dion said, tipping his beer in Aidan's direction. "Trust me, you'll love the other side of this."

Aidan nodded to his friend, his partner, and the man who'd had his back more times than he could count. "You'll be my best man, right?"

"Only if I say yes," Gail interjected, bringing his attention back to her.

"Will you?"

"Will I what?"

"Say yes?" Aidan said.

With a huge sigh, Gail settled her hands on Aidan's shoulder. "I don't know, sweetheart."

What? She needed to think about it? Aidan's heart plummeted. He thought he'd figured it out. Thought he knew her and how she felt. "Why not?"

"Because, you silly man," Gail said with a smile. "You still haven't asked me a question."

He hadn't asked a— Of course, he had. Hadn't he? No, maybe not. Still, it had been inferred. The woman was going to make him completely debase himself, huh? Well, two could play at that game.

He smiled at her, the Aidan smile that had always gotten him where he wanted to go before. "All right, doll. You want me to ask? I'll ask."

Aidan stood, pulling her up with him to cradle her in his arms, then he kissed her. Kissed her like he'd meant to after she accepted his proposal. His tongue touched her lips and she opened to him.

After long moments held in her spell, Aidan released her, happy with the dazed expression he could see on her face. "I dare you to marry me, Gail Grayson. Will you?" He whispered words meant only for them.

"Yes. I believe I will be quite happy to take that dare," she breathed back.

He'd tried to be quiet, but the whooping and hollering behind them belied the attempt.

All he had time for was a quick peck before they were pulled away and into the congratulatory arms of Dion and Claire, and Hawk and Julia.

"This calls for champagne," Julia said. "And sparkling cider for us, eh, Gail?"

With an apologetic look toward Aidan, Gail followed the women into the kitchen.

Dion and Hawk both clapped Aidan on the back, almost drawing the breath out of his chest. "Congratulations, man," they each said. "Well done."

And just like that, everything in Aidan's life fell into place. He'd found the one thing he'd been searching for all his life. Home.

Aidan smiled and accepted the shot of whiskey Hawk handed him. "You're going to need this, what with having a pregnant fiancée," Hawk said.

Aidan laughed with both of them, but set the drink down. He and Gail would walk this path together. Especially now that the threat was neutralized.

"Thank you," he said to Dion.

"For what?"

"For taking care of that asshole." Aidan would have loved to pull the trigger himself, but Dion's quick action had saved his life. "I owe you, man."

Dion pulled him into a quick man-hug. "No more than I owe you."

Hawk lifted his drink to them. "All three of us have reasons to be grateful for our friendship."

Aidan laughed. "You say that now. A few months ago, when you were trying to keep us from arresting you for piracy, I'm betting you didn't feel the same."

"No," Hawk said with a laugh, then glanced toward the kitchen with a warm expression. "But I can't fault how it turned out. For any of us."

"I couldn't agree more," Aidan said, knowing his life had been forever changed and he didn't mind it a bit.

CHAPTER TWENTY-FIVE

Champagne got passed around, then dinner served, and it was the longest night of Gail's life. All she wanted was to be alone with her husband-to-be. He hadn't handed her a ring yet, but she didn't care. The commitment was there, along with a love that would last forever.

Now, finally alone, worry filled her as they walked up the stairs to her apartment. Aidan was fidgeting, something he never did. Was he having second thoughts?

Gail's heart hit the floor. She knew without a doubt that if Aidan left, if he couldn't match her commitment to him, that it would feel worse than her kidnapping, worse than his beating. It would crush her.

Aidan took the keys from her shaking hands and opened the apartment door. "I should probably tell you something," he said. His voice shook.

Gail felt the dread of a thousand deaths fill her. She couldn't do this. Not out here on the landing. She needed to be inside where she could sit down. She pushed the door open and rushed inside to her bedroom, where she froze.

In between her tightly fit bed and dresser now lay a bassinet, fully assembled and awash in pink. Pink? She was barely pregnant. How could he—

Aidan wrapped his arms around her, covering her belly with his hands. "I know we don't know the sex of the baby yet, but I hope it's a girl. I can hardly wait to see her spiky dark hair and chocolate eyes. To lose sleep gazing at this little doll we made. To love you even more than I do now, if that's even possible, as we raise our family."

"You're...you're not leaving me?"

Aidan's eyes widened. "God, no. You're my life. How could you even think that?"

"Your voice...you said we needed to talk...out on the landing..." She sniffled as she turned in his arms.

"I only wanted to warn you. I've heard it's not good to surprise a pregnant woman," Aidan said with a devilish grin on his face.

"It's not," Gail answered immediately. "And don't you forget it."

"I'll try not to. So, what would you think about me being around more?"

"You mean, like moving in?"

Aidan glanced around. "This place isn't big enough. We'll have to find something else."

"But you live in England."

"Well, maybe not for much longer. Turns out, my boss wants to set up a branch office." He could feel her breath catch and hold. "Breathe, baby. Just breathe."

Air whooshed out of Gail's lungs. "In San Diego?"

"It's already in the works. And he needs someone to head it up."

"Y-you?"

Aidan grinned into her hair. "If I want it, the job's mine."

"Do you? Want it, I mean? Wouldn't you miss the field work?"

"Maybe. But there's more excitement in my life right here than I could ever find in the underbelly of humanity. I think it might just be time to leave that behind. After all, I'm about to be a family man." He pushed out his chest, mirroring the pride he now felt at that idea.

"Yes, you are. Husband, father, lover..." Gail turned in his arms, her eyes glowing with obvious pride and happiness.

"So you think you can handle me being around full time, then?" Aidan asked.

"Oh, I think that's a distinct possibility. No more worrying about where you are and when you'll be home. No more waiting by the phone."

"Still, there's something to be said for phone sex."

"A good reason but not good enough. I'd rather have you here, in the flesh."

"I hoped you'd say that, because I've already pretty much accepted the job."

"Yay!" Gail hollered. "Aidan, I'm not sure I could be any happier than I am at this moment."

"Me, either," he said, smoothing her hair with his hand and staring into eyes he wanted to see for the rest of his life.

"Although..." Gail said.

"What?"

"Well, I just don't know what we'll do with all this pink if it's a boy."

Aidan buried his head in her neck for a long moment before pulling back and kissing her. "If it's a boy, then we'll just have to save this for the next one, or the next, or the next."

"I think, Mr. Walker, that I am quite fine with that." Gail kissed him back.

"I know I've got a lot to learn," Aidan said. "I'm going to make mistakes."

"Me, too." Gail pulled his head down to hers. "Let's learn together."

"That, Future Mrs. Walker, is the sexiest thing you've said yet."

Thank you for reading **Dare to Love,** the sequel to *Pirate's Promise* and the final story in this trilogy. If you enjoyed this book, please consider leaving an honest review wherever you prefer, and know that it would be greatly appreciated.

There's a sneak preview of Rudy's Heart, a standalone Montana ranch romance, at the end of this book. And be sure to check out more of Laurie Ryan's books at:

www.laurieryanauthor.com

For new release information and news about Laurie Ryan, please sign up for her newsletter.

BOOKS BY LAURIE RYAN

Contemporary Romance stories

<u>Billionaire Bachelor Pledge series</u>

Royal Flush

High Card

All In

Full House

Blind Bet

<u>Willow Bay series</u>

Last Resort

Finding Home

Chances Are

Tender Tide

Reluctant Christmas

Operation Ethan

<u>Tropical Persuasions series</u>

Stolen Treasures

Pirate's Promise

Dare to Love

Standalone

The Long Journey Home

Rudy's Heart

Lost and Found

Northern Lights

Healing Love

Women's Fiction

Show Me

Fantasy

Survival

Enlightenment

Birthright

Awakening

Wolf's Call

ABOUT THE AUTHOR

Laurie Ryan writes about resilient, independent women who might stumble, but they dust themselves off and get the job done. Their men, whether commanding alpha or endearing cinnamon roll heroes, will do whatever it takes to ensure the happiness of the women they cherish.

Laurie lives in the Pacific Northwest with her "he can fix anything" hubby, but is always willing to travel to visit their children and grandchildren. Her creativity isn't limited to writing. She also scrap books and, when she really needs to disappear, she paints rocks and shells found on the beaches she walks at the ocean—her happy place.

Laurie has always had a deep connection to nature and the outdoors, which is reflected in her writing. She is a passionate writer who brings her love for nature, animals, and creativity into her work.

An avid cruiser, Laurie has visited many places. One of her favorites was a stop in Greenland, where the strength and endurance of the people living in those beautiful but harsh surroundings became an underlying thread in her stories. Her sensual romance novels are sure to warm the hearts of readers.

Connect with Laurie on Facebook, Instagram, or TikTok, or her website, and join Laurie's newsletter for up to date news and releases.

Laurie loves to hear from her readers and can be reached at laurie@laurieryanauthor.com

SNEAK PREVIEW

RUDY'S HEART

By Laurie Ryan

The Story

An uncle-turned-father, terrified he'll screw up, enlists the help of a burned-out, empathic woman with an oh-so-rightful chip on her shoulder.□

Emotionally shattered from her hospice work, Aubrey Gannet journeys to a Montana ranch looking for peace and quiet to rekindle her grieving spirit. But will she be able to forgive the man who deserted his only sister when she needed him the most?

Stuck with an angry horse no one can get near and a child

who refuses to speak, loner Beck Hawthorne is desperate to get through to them and hoping Aubrey Gannet holds that key. Only together can they break the bonds of sadness and find a brighter future.

Emotional. Sensual. Standalone. A romance novel that includes a wonderfully intuitive horse named Rudy and a six-year-old who will wrap herself around your heart. #contemporaryromance #horseranch #montana

SNEAK PEEK

Chapter One

Tail flying high, the horse raced to the far end of the corral and reared when the fence prevented his escape. He whirled around, kicking at fence boards that bounced with the force of the blow but withstood the battering. Once, twice, three times he kicked. When he finally dropped to four legs, he stood there shivering, his coat glossy with sweat.

Beck Hawthorne settled a booted foot on the lowest board and leaned on the fence, wondering for the thousandth time in the last month why he'd taken on this horse. Brought to Beck from an abusive situation, Rudy wouldn't let a soul near him. He'd bitten two of Beck's men and tried to kick a third when they'd moved him from the trailer to this corral. When they'd tried to bathe him, he'd fought until they were forced to stop or risk injury, to the horse or to them. Rudy had been so terrified, Beck couldn't put him through that again. Now, Beck wouldn't let any of his men near the horse. He alone set out food and mucked out the lean-to at the end of the corral, the one they'd built so Rudy would have more shade and a place to eat. Not that he'd gotten any thanks for it. Nope. Nothing but angry puffs of air from the far side of the corral whenever he entered with food or pitchfork. Rudy ate the feed, but only after Beck retreated from sight.

How could he get through to this animal? Everything he'd tried so far had dismal results. And now his young niece seemed taken with the horse. Damn it. Beck slapped the fence and the horse jumped even with the distance between them. He yanked his hat off and wiped sweat from his brow with his arm.

"Beck?"

Cassidy, the face of Hope Ranch and Beck's go-to for all things organizational, stood several feet back, toying with a strand of kinky hair that had four or five colors woven through it, colors that complemented her dark skin. She eyed the horse as she held out a phone. "Mara's asking for you and won't take no for an answer."

Mara. His favorite cousin, even if she was a royal pain in the ass. Okay, his only cousin. With a last glance at the horse, Beck thanked Cassidy and took the phone.

"Hey, Mars."

"Yeah, and that nickname never gets old," she drawled. "How's my favorite little girl doing?"

Dani. The niece he'd been given sole custody of. The worry knot in Beck's throat tightened. "She's no better, no worse. She's healthy, fed, seems content. I just can't get her to open up, to tell me how to help her."

"Give it time," Mara said. "It hasn't been that long."

"It's been months."

"Not very many, though. Grief takes its own time. She'll let you know when she's ready to talk. In the meantime, just love her and let her enjoy the ranch. By the way, where the heck were you hiding? I could have painted my nails and dried them in the time it took your assistant to find you."

"I live on a ranch now, remember? Nothing's a short walk. You know that." He nodded to Cassidy, thinking that would act as a dismissal, but she stayed where she was. Beck should have known better. His ranch manager's daughter kept this place running smoothly, though her attitude got a bit proprietary at times.

"Yes, dear cousin, I do," Mara said. "Speaking of which, how's everything going?"

Beck headed back toward the house. When Cassidy fell in step beside him, he glared at her, but he knew she wouldn't budge. If she wasn't so good at her job ...

"Things are slow," he told Mara. She had a right to know. She'd been there to help for the first couple weeks after he'd bought the place. "The barn is ready and I'm searching for the right quarter horses to begin the breeding program. Since it could take years for that to be profitable, I hope to bring in several hundred head of cattle this fall, which means we're working on fencing."

"And the house?"

"The bed and breakfast is a low priority, but it's coming along."

"Good, because I've got your first customer, a woman I know."

"Mars, we're not open yet." The B&B idea had been Cassidy's. Beck had thought her nuts, but anything that would make some money for the pit into which he'd sunk a huge chunk of his finances couldn't be a bad idea, right? Now, he was back to thinking it was crazy.

"It will be a good run-through for the guest part of your ranch. And she'll be no trouble. She just needs a place to rest for a while."

Rest? How old was this woman? "Absolutely not. I don't even have the rooms furnished yet. The furniture doesn't arrive for another two weeks."

"Then move a bed, dresser, and chair from the bunkhouse to that room at the front. It's the quietest and has the best view."

Instantly, Beck regretted Mara's visit to the ranch after his niece came to live with him. She'd been a huge help, but the woman remembered too much.

"Come on, Beckett. She needs a break and you need a test guest. It's a win-win."

The sting of hearing that name punched Beck in the gut. He hadn't gone by that in years. Since college, to be exact. Since his father, Beckett, Sr., had died, along with Beck's mother. Beckett brought back too many memories, some of which were tied to fresh wounds.

"We could bring furniture up, but— "

"Good, because her name is Aubrey Gannet and she's already on her way."

"What?"

"Yep. I saw her off this morning. Figured you'd come around and recognize the benefit for both of you. She's driving from Seattle and isn't a speedy traveler, so it'll be three days before she arrives. She won't stay long. I promise. Just a few days."

Great. Some old woman who drove fifty miles per hour on the freeway. Beck pictured her on Montana's highways, a line of traffic honking behind her. "That's not enough time," he told Mara.

"Sure it is. But Becky?"

And there it was. The other name he preferred to never hear again. He hated that childhood name, gifted to him by the one and only Mara. If she weren't the one person he could count on, he'd give her an earful.

"Take it easy on her, okay? She's had it rough and really needs to rest."

"Who are you sending me? Someone who's sick or something?"

"Not sick. Tired."

Great. Not only a guest he wasn't ready for, but a guest with issues. Beck glanced back at Rudy, who'd moved to his fresh food. In the opposite direction, Dani stared through a window, another lost soul, her eyes riveted on that damn horse. The look of longing on her face was something Beck didn't need words to decipher. Grief had turned his six-year-old niece into a silent ball of sadness. She seemed lonely, too, though she was rarely alone. Now, some old lady who'd probably need more help than Mara thought was on her way to join them. From Seattle. Where Dani had lived until coming to live with him.

Somehow, he'd become a home for wounded souls. Beck clicked off the call with Mara and handed the phone to Cassidy, who'd kept pace with him.

"It seems we're about to have company. Have someone bring up the best bed and dresser from the bunkhouse and put it in the front bedroom upstairs."

"Who's coming?"

"I have no idea. Mara sent her. Some lady who needs to rest. Apparently, we've turned into a recovery home for the aged. And the young. And horses."

~~~

"What have you gotten me into?" Aubrey Gannet muttered, and not for the first time, to the woman listening on the other end of the phone, the culprit behind her predicament.

"This will be good for you," Mara said. "You need to get away for a while."

"I need to relax, not disappear. I just left Butte, and it already seems like I'm in the middle of nowhere." She'd left her comfort zone way behind. It had been a while since she'd traveled anywhere except to visit patients, and now, she was two states away from home and lost. It had taken her until well past noon to find the motivation to get going, which left zero time to un-lose herself. "Plus, didn't you say it would be temperate this time of year?"

A sheen of sweat covered the tops of her hands and her palms stuck to the steering wheel. Aubrey peeled them off and wiped them, one at a time, on her jeans. Sweat was her nervous release, though it generally made matters worse rather
~~~

than better. Still, today was sweltering. Her old car overheat-ed without much convincing. Not wanting to break down on the far side of nowhere, she'd opted for windows-down air conditioning, though that resulted in the scent of sun-baked everything permeating the air inside her car.

"If there's nothing around you, you must be close, which means you're going to lose cell service soon."

"Lose cell service?" Oh, this was so going from bad to worse.

"Yes ... remember ... relax and don't ... anyone ask you ... help. Tell ... him ... be nice. Goodb— "

With that unfinished word, Aubrey's cell cut out, apparently for the duration of her visit to Nowhere, Montana.

Running a hand along her neck, Aubrey yanked her pony-tail, a miserable failure at keeping her cooler, over her shoul-der. She sighed. How had Mara talked her into this? A week ago, she'd shown up at Aubrey's apartment with a bottle of wine. By the end of that bottle, she'd elicited a promise from Aubrey—a mandatory vacation—and had held her to it. Her friend had taken total advantage of her moment of weakness.

Aubrey needed a break. She knew that. Too much death had visited her of late. Normally, she handled that a lot better. As a hospice social worker, she considered it an extraordinary priv-ilege to help patients cross that final threshold in as peace-filled a way as possible. That never used to get to her. Hope's passing had broken her, though. Work, life, everything – it all seemed so futile.

Hope Jones, the dark-haired, thirty-one-year-old with brown, soulful eyes, had handled her cancer with quiet calmness, her entire focus on her young daughter. Seeing that relationship, Aubrey had longed for her own family, her own children.

Then Hope died and the little girl drew into herself. Nothing Aubrey did brought the girl out of her shell. She'd tried over several days to help the silent sadness in the six-year-old's face, to no avail. Aubrey had considered trying to fast-track a foster-parent application.

That's when the child had disappeared. Whisked away by some relative Hope had only mentioned once, and even then, she'd barely said anything. A brother. He'd never come to visit Hope in the months Aubrey had been part of her life. And Hope's no-account ex-husband had disappeared before the positive symbol on the pregnancy test had become clear. Hope had confided in Aubrey that the man had sent papers giving up all his rights to his daughter in the same envelope as the divorce papers.

Had Hope asked her no-account brother to take the child? Aubrey had a hard time believing she would do that. Aubrey had tried to find the six-year-old. No matter how much Aubrey begged child services, no one would tell her where the brother lived. Even Mara, the girl's cousin, had been close-mouthed, giving Aubrey some cockamamie story that she needed to heal herself first.

After that, her job became more burden than blessing. She'd tried to give her patients the best care, to hide her tears for the families and friends. She'd buried her own emotions pretty well, she'd thought. Until her boss put her on a mandatory leave of absence.

"Get your head back in the game and your heart out of it." Gwen said the words with gentle effect, and then reminded Aubrey how good she was at hospice work and that they'd hate to lose her.

"Burnout is real," Gwen said.

So, after two weeks of Aubrey barely sleeping and eating, Mara had shown up at her door.

Aubrey glared at the semi-arid, empty landscape passing by her car window. Friend or no friend, when she got home, she would pound Mara.

After another mile, fenced fields appeared on both sides of the road. Then, finally, the typical tall wooden and metal structure that heralded the entrance to a ranch. Aubrey turned off the road and stopped. A mailbox had the name Hawthorne on it. That's the name Mara had given her. Her gaze moved up to the sign swaying in the welcome breeze.

Hope Ranch.

Aubrey's heart pounded, her hand the only thing keeping it from thumping right out of her chest. The name brought all the pain and grief, never far from her mind, roaring to the forefront. She looked at the address Mara gave her. The same numbers were screwed to the fence post in front of her. This was the right place.

Had Mara known? Aubrey swiped at the tears that fell unbidden. Hope. Too young to have her life snuffed out. The pain was real. Her gut spasmed as she thought of the last moments in her friend's life. And now the grief surged, being here, at a place with her friend's name on the front gate. She got out of the car and walked to the fence, looking each way at the long stretch of board and post that followed the road until she couldn't see it anymore. Her hand hovered over the wood for a long moment before resting on its roughness.

Hope.

I miss you so much.

How had Mara found this place? Sent her here? Aubrey couldn't do this. Couldn't stay where everything would be wrapped around memories of her lost friend. She got in her car, resolute about turning around, heading back to Butte. Grabbing the steering wheel, she leaned forward and rested her forehead on her hands.

It hurt so much. Everything hurt. How was she ever going to be happy again?

She gazed up at the stylized sign, remembering how Hope had whiled away hours with pen and paper in her hand, doodling those same types of curly-cues. She'd gifted Aubrey with one of her pages of doodles. Tesla would have been proud of the freehand designs. And she treasured the gift, which lay framed and safely tucked in her suitcase.

If she turned around and went home, she'd have to listen to Mara's consternation for days or weeks on end. Maybe she should spend a night, check it out. Then, Mara would get off her case and she could get back to the rightful depression she'd been mired in.

The sun was well on its way down the westward path to setting, so she might not make it back to Butte by nightfall. Driving solo on a pitch-black, lonely road wasn't a smart choice. So be it. Aubrey straightened. One night. Anything could be tolerated for one night, right? She started the engine and, since she only had a short way to go, she put the windows up and turned on the blessed air conditioning.

As she headed down the winding driveway, she followed fencing that separated pastures into a perfect, idyllic setting, just like in the movies. This ranch used blond wood fencing that seemed to melt into the view, not stand out. It looked right. On one side, several horses stood, enjoying the late afternoon heat. One neighed, making Aubrey smile as she remembered riding all those years ago. She'd planned to have her own horses by twenty, but life had taken her in a more urban direction. Living in Seattle had left no room for equestrian hobbies. As she neared the ranch house, Aubrey noticed a lone horse in a fenced area on the other side. Aubrey squinted to get a better view in the sunshine. A brown and white, very dirty horse watched her with troubled, soulful eyes while she drove past.

She parked in front of a two-story, sprawling house. Having never been on a ranch before, Aubrey only had movies to guide her perception. This didn't stray far from those ideals. With a wrap-around porch and siding that looked like reclaimed barn wood, it didn't look old. Rather, it looked homey, with brushes of color in standing and hanging flower pots. Chairs, gliders, and small tables dotted the porch and an American flag hung from a small post jutting out above white-washed stairs that invited you to enter.

Stepping out of the car, Aubrey took a deep breath. At that moment, as she gazed around, peace filled her to the point she didn't want to move. To stay here, to feel a tranquility foreign to her these days, was a blessing. Aubrey closed her eyes and turned her face to the sun, accepting the heat as part of what made this moment feel good.

She couldn't stand there forever, though, so she popped the trunk and pulled out her suitcase, closing it quietly. She didn't want to disturb the serenity. Before she headed inside to locate someone, she looked back at the lone horse. He stood on the far side of the pasture and she could see him shivering. She set her suitcase down, her feet drawn toward the fence, her eyes focused on the horse. Something had hurt him. She could sense the pain, feel the fear.

The horse held her gaze as she reached for the wood fence slat. She stood there, silent and still, waiting. It took a while, but the horse stepped in her direction, moving toward her like one of those slow-motion commercials with Clydesdales. Except this was no workhorse. This boy was sleek and dappled in the white and brown striations of a pinto. Aubrey couldn't remember anything or anyone looking as handsome as this guy, even though the matting and mud-caking of his hair had turned the white patches to a dull gray.

The strangest sensation filled her as the horse got closer, as if she was coming home. When the horse stopped in front of her, Aubrey reached out her hand.

"Stop!"

***

More information about this story and more by Laurie Ryan can be found on her website.